la femme

la femme

Edited by Ian Whates

NEWCON
PRESS

NewCon Press
England

First edition, published in the UK April 2014
by NewCon Press

NCP 070 (hardback)
NCP 071 (softback)

10 9 8 7 6 5 4 3 2 1

ISBN: 978-1-907069-66-6 (hardback)
978-1-907069-67-3 (softback)

Front cover photograph of Adele Kirby © Pam Martin
Back cover photograph of Adele Kirby © Shaun Hodge
Cover design and layout by Andy Bigwood

Text layout by Storm Constantine

Contents

La Femme: An Introduction

Ian Whates

Sometimes a story can take you by surprise, but it's rare for an anthology to do so, especially when you're the person responsible for compiling it. Yet in essence that's what happened here.

You see, I was merrily commissioning and editing stories for an anthology themed round the femme fatale which swiftly expanded to encompass 'women who are more or less than they seem', when something strange happened. The submissions were being stubborn. I had some great stories here, but they refused to marry together into a coherent collection. In fact, it became increasingly clear that what I had was two collections struggling to fit into one skin. Eventually, bowing to the inevitable, I separated them and gave the two books their freedom, which is how the duo anthology came into being: *La Femme* and its sister volume *Noir.*

Some of the authors in *La Femme* will be familiar to NewCon readers: Stephen Palmer, who appeared in *Further Conflicts*, Storm Constantine whose fiction I've been delighted to feature in several titles and Andrew Hook likewise, while Holly Ice made her NewCon debut in last year's *Looking Landwards*. Others, perhaps less so…

It was Adrian Tchaikovsky who first recommended Frances Hardinge to me, while Tricia Sullivan suggested I look at the work of Benjanun Sriduangkaew – and I'm extremely grateful in both instances, particularly given the quality of story that has resulted. Ruth EJ Booth actually submitted her piece for a different project entirely, but I felt it to be better suited here, while Jonathan Oliver and I experience a switch of roles. As head honcho of Solaris, Jon was responsible for editing my *Noise* novels. Stewart Hotston and I fell into conversation at a convention last year, where I discovered he used to be a quantum physicist. Well, naturally I wanted a story from him. I've known both Maura McHugh and John Llewellyn Probert for a while, admiring their writing and, in John's case, the quality of his superbly witty dramatic productions at various cons. Maura has theatrical connections too, and I still regret not making it into London to see the production of *The Hallowe'en Sessions*, which she co-wrote with Kim Newman, Paul McAuley, Anne Bilson and Stephen Volk. I've long wanted to work with both Maura and John, and *La Femme* offered the perfect opportunity. Then, of course, there's Adele Kirby, who has the unique privilege (at least as far as NewCon Press is concerned) of appearing on both the front and back covers of the book and within its pages. Adele's submission proved a delightful surprise: a far future romance of sweeping scope and ambition.

These are the twelve contributors who collectively produced *La Femme*, a volume of stories that, hopefully, will hold as many surprises for the reader as it did for the editor.

Ian Whates
February 2014
Cambridgeshire

Palestinian Sweets

Stephen Palmer

Lucas Nohandys sensed the existence of people long departed as he walked through the scent-fossils of Wardour Street. This thoroughfare, the heart of West Jerusalem, was for him a miasma of information, a cloud, from which he could acquire knowledge transmitted in computer-generated biochemical format. A dog, they called him. It was quite a compliment.

At the end of Wardour Street lay the heart of Greek Orthodoxy, the restaurant known as the Status Quo, where his family lived; where his nose was based, and his other nose too. But tonight a new customer would present herself, a woman from the other side: Randa, negotiator, whose second name was unknown.

It was early evening, June. The time had come for the tussle.

Lucas was small, black-haired and slim, and he slipped beneath the scent barrier of the Status Quo's front door without setting off the alarm – the restaurant's computers knew his sweat. Yes, he had eaten garlic, but that could be compensated for. More difficult were the complications of the traditional Palestinian meal musakhan, whose allspice and pine nuts could come from anywhere in the tropical world. But the restaurant was quiet, the night-time rush yet to begin. He heard the creak of floorboards upstairs as his family finished their own meal. He heard the beep of an olfactor, smelled the drifting fug of retsina.

His mother, Irene. emerged from the doorway at the bottom of the stairs. "So you've come back in one piece."

Lucas shrugged. "Enemies are for children. I'm a man."

"You'll be telling me next you're some kind of negotiator."

Lucas scowled. From the steam-washed air he pulled information: molecules of ash, molecules of leaf. "So your boyfriend was here earlier. Did you tell Father?"

"We have an open marriage now. How many times do I have to tell you that?"

Lucas looked away. Conflict disturbed him. Was that why he remained in London long after the British had departed for their green countryside? "You know," he said, "this family doesn't have to stay here. We could return to Israel."

Irene chortled. "Who wants to go back there? I like the cosmopolitan life. I like London as it is now. You forget, Lucas, I was here when the embassy patchwork started. I remember."

"I haven't forgotten that." He turned to walk away. "But what a shame Father is so much younger than you and can't remember."

"Did you get them?"

Lucas glanced at his father, then turned back to the window and gazed out across London Central. "No."

"What happened?" Zeid asked.

Lucas took a handful of bizir al-bateekh and threw them into his open mouth, the seeds squidging against his teeth as he chewed. He sighed.

"You didn't give us away, Lucas?"

Lucas shook his head. His father walked to his side. Lucas stared at the distant line of faux-Himalayas, soft white with a hint of pink, in the distance where Marble Arch used to be, and he shook his head again. Half a world away.

"Tell me," said Zeid.

"The woman was there."

"The one making eyes at you?"

"Yeah, that one. Ghinwa. She was with her brother all afternoon so I didn't get anywhere near him. He must still have the packet of sweets on him."

Zeid nodded. "There's still plenty of time. Randa isn't due here for a few hours."

"But what are we going to do? Mother will be suspicious-"

"Mother is too busy with her toy boy. We can forget your mother."

Lucas sighed. "Yeah. Of course we can. So what's your plan?"

"The Palestinians want us to receive those sweets. All we have to do is get the sister out of the way. Maybe… maybe I should be the recipient."

"But I'm the negotiator. What would I be doing?"

"Making sweet love to Ghinwa. Her name means song. So sing to her."

Lucas said nothing. In this city of broken quarters anything was possible for an ambassador. But what song could he sing? His record of success (he hated that word) with women was poor, as his father – his loving, supportive father – had observed on numerous occasions. But then, as his father also observed, no man in this family had much luck with women, for obvious reasons.

"Just wine her and seduce her with knowledge," Zeid continued. "You know how to do that, don't you? And don't feel bad. Cultural relations have no remit of love. You were born into this family, and that's that. Listen, Lucas, I'm proud you became a negotiator, it would've been so easy for you to return to the West Bank."

"Sure. Easy. My life – easy. Yeah."

"Go now. Don't make a plan – if you do she'll smell you're faking. Improvise. And don't forget, for women, the nipples-"

"Father! I am sixteen."

The Jameed was well known to Lucas: a restaurant in an alley off Baker Street, this was the centre of Palestinian Christianity in London. Those braided scent-lines that crossed Hindu-controlled Oxford Street were like delicate silk threads spun by the fattest, most decadent spiders, that had dined on apricot jam and dibs. Those lines were a map of the locale, experienced by Lucas in complex synchrony with the information being transmitted by his optic nerves. As a negotiator he had the right to enter the Jameed, and even eat there, so long as he had been invited. Similarly, Randa ("scented tree") had the right to eat free and easy in the Status Quo. But women were something else for the nosy man, something else entirely.

The matter of the Palestinian's Schism was becoming complex.

Stress: the belief that you are in danger. Yes, he was stressed, denying as much was pointless and dangerous. Luckily this stress worked against his heart, not his digestive system – the possibly fatal flaw of the Nohandys family, whose male line had lost so many to cardiac arrest.

His heart beat quickly as he slipped beneath the scent barrier of the Jameed's front door without setting off the alarm – the restaurant's computers knew his sweat. Inside, six o'clock, a few Palestinian diners from Jerusalem and a Jewish couple, but elsewhere the building was quiet, lit only by green-glowing algae tubes. No candles of course – stink of burning.

At the rear of the dining area he saw a shadow move within a greater shadow. He smelled information: Ghinwa, her skin scent obvious, and the musky, almost Gaza Strip odour of her brother Amin.

"You're back?"

He ignored Amin's question, knowing Zeid was nearby.

Ghinwa was an olive-skinned beauty, long black hair scented with grape blossom, dark eyes, tall and slim. "The source of much jasmine is Egypt," he told her.

She smiled. He guessed she liked him. The smile was sincere. And that code phrase rooted in the twentieth century perfume industry meant no living mannequin moulded by plastic surgery and sprayed with Greek Orthodoxy had entered her restaurant.

"Hi Lucas," she said. "You just can't keep away, can you?"

Lucas shrugged. "This is such an important time for our little bit of the patchwork."

She approached him, then stepped aside to lean against the bar. "Na'ana tea or maramiyyeh?"

Lucas did not care for sage. "Na'ana."

Amin stared at him, the slightest hint of desperation in his eyes.

Lucas whispered to Ghinwa, "I'm lonely."

He had no idea what he was saying. It popped out, as the truth so often does. She stopped breathing for a moment, as if her brain was computing the message of the two words. She seemed to have no idea what he was saying. "Really?"

He nodded. "And a little bored. Are you?"

"Lucas, I mean… Lucas, I didn't guess…"

He shrugged. "We get so few opportunities to chat. But you're beautiful, I have noticed." He paused, almost empty of inspiration. "Do you think you're beautiful?"

"What a question to ask a girl!"

He said nothing, looking into her eyes, as if demanding through the force of his silence that she confront, then answer his question.

She murmured, "I have been told –"

"No, what do you think?"

She glanced to her left, then at the floor, then over her shoulder at her brother; uncomfortable, he knew, but he needed this hold over her, this unexpected thing that he had snatched, unsmelled, from the chemistry between them.

He smiled. "Ghinwa, you like me!"

"Oh, well…"

And she blushed.

Lucas knew this moment was a unique moment that he could not waste, and he took her by the hand and moved forward, so that his right hip touched her belly; then he brushed his lips against hers. Her mouth stayed closed, yet he smelled her surprised pleasure, and he knew her pheromones were changing in response to the kiss. But this was the toughest part for a negotiator: the art of sincerity.

She pulled back. "But Lucas… you're Greek Orthodox."

"I know. You're Palestinian, and we're fighting." He shrugged.

She glanced down at the floor again. "Not fighting exactly…"

"As good as. This is religion. Religion's composed of fighting."

It was almost as if she remembered with horror that her brother sat a few metres away. With a gasp she turned around… then breathed out. He saw her shoulders relax, as if a weight had been removed from them. Amin was looking the other way as he poured water into a plant pot.

Lucas knew that the moment was gone now, though secure, and that neither of them would forget it. He felt something for Ghinwa. But he prayed in the silence of his mind that he had given his father enough time.

The sweets were extraordinary, the like of them never seen before.

In Lucas' room at the Status Quo, Zeid frowned. "But these are like mughli." He sniffed one, then added, "Condensed mughli."

Lucas looked at his father then shrugged.

"Sweets prepared to celebrate a newborn child," Zeid explained. Lucas heard the confusion in his voice. "It's a dessert made of ground rice, sugar and a mixture of spices, garnished with almonds, pine nuts and walnuts. But what is the newborn child we're expecting?"

"Is this a Schism matter?"

Zeid sat back. After a few moments he said, "It must be. Why else would the Palestinians send these to us?"

Lucas glanced up at the horologique on the wall. Randa would be here in an hour.

"What game are they playing?" Zeid said. "Is this intended to confuse us? Distract us?"

"Or do I actually eat one?"

Zeid stared at him, and, horrified, Lucas realised that his father had not considered this possibility.

He continued, "Father, you thought I was only meant to sniff them?"

Zeid pressed the silver foil back around the column of sweets and threw the packet into a polythene container. "Computer! Clean the air."

There came the subliminal sound of air cleansers doing their work, pumping out molecule traps into the room atmosphere. Lucas grimaced. Unavoidably, the London-standardised cleansers had their own odour, which made him nauseous; they smelled of south of the river.

Zeid said, "Smelling information in patchwork London is all very well, but eating something from another side is different."

"It's something to get emotional about."

Zeid's expression was puzzled.

"You've never negotiated, Father. It's a dry, scholarly affair. Afterwards I always feel the need to jump up and down and shout, or punch somebody, or hug somebody. Negotiating is like chess. Thank God I never learned to play that. Yeah, it's like chess, all brains and no love."

"You need to snap out of this slightly self-pitying mood," Zeid said, standing up. "Pull yourself together. Let's go downstairs and prepare the restaurant." He glanced at the horologique. "We're open in half an hour."

"But what about the sweets?"

"For now we'll have to leave them. Mughli... no, that's too risky. There's a message there for us but I can't read it. Can you?"

"No."

Zeid nodded. "We take no risks here. We don't want the Palestinians getting one over on us. We didn't find out about the existence of these sweets by accident."

Lucas followed his father downstairs. The waiters and waitresses were all present, Naga the cook too; to all intents and purposes it was a normal night that would be filled with normal food.

The taste of Ghinwa on his lips just wouldn't go away.

Randa the scented tree looked much like Ghinwa the song – tall and slim, but with long brown hair instead of black; the same Mediterranean skin and the same sultry eyes. She wore the standard neutral garb of a negotiator.

Lucas also wore work clothes: charcoal grey trousers and jacket, white shirt tied not buttoned, white socks, black shoes. The clothes were made of a fabric to which scent molecules could not stick, designed by UNHCR scientists in the years following the Lebanese Bomb; the same scientists who created the biochemical format. Lucas disliked these clothes because they spoke of conformity, but he liked them because they suggested influence, even power.

He was the soul of the planet, after all – he and all his comrades in this intense city. He was a pheromone-haunted executor of humanity. Let the others play with their silly electronic toys. Knowledge... that went deeper. The others had information, but here in London Central there was knowledge, and, perhaps, wisdom.

"The source of much ja..." He halted, realising that without thinking he had almost used Ghinwa's security. He shuddered. Randa would have been offended, worsening the Schism between the churches. "A molecule of lemon scent is identical to a molecule of orange scent, but formed in mirror image."

Randa nodded. Though she was the visitor, the stranger in this restaurant of mezedes and retsina, she was a woman, deferential to the man. Lucas saw contempt of his masculinity in her expression.

An opening gambit, he told himself. She doesn't mean it. She's a tool of Palestinian Christianity. She probably likes me. She's not as pretty as Ghinwa though –

He pulled himself back into the real world. Leading her to the table assigned for the negotiation he first pulled back one of the two chairs, inviting her to sit, then sat opposite her. Behind him stood a wall (he had the right to this because he was on home territory) but behind Randa lay the entire ground floor of the restaurant – twenty one tables, algae tube lamps, pictures of faux-waterfalls like they had in Indian restaurants, and the bar, the well-stocked bar, full of retsina, ouzo, Mythos beer, tsipouro, tentura and metaxa. And of course a frappé machine. Already customers were arriving; the night promised to be busy.

Randa had put her briefcase on the floor before sitting, but now she lifted it up and placed it to her right. Lucas followed suit, taking the briefcase earlier prepared and placing it to his left. He tapped the algae lamp between them. It responded to his touch, and the circulating filaments of blue-green brightened, lending a marine cast to the table.

"Welcome to the Status Quo, scented tree," he said.

Randa nodded, but did not meet his gaze.

"Are you ready to order?" he asked.

"Yes." Her voice was deep for a woman, and husky, as if she smoked argeelah. "Yes, let's begin without delay."

Lucas clicked his fingers at the knot of waiters beside the bar and made play of studying the menu. He had long before decided on his strategy and knew exactly what to order, though it would of course depend on what she ordered, this being an affair of thrust and counter-thrust. Randa did not bother to look at him. She knew he was acting out the formal requirements of the negotiation. Her manner, typical of the Palestinians, was world weary. She pushed locks of hair behind her ears, the better to frame her face.

"I'll have the piperies," she told the waiter.

Lucas nodded. This piperies orektiko was a standard starter, a choice neutral through its variety, indicating willingness to proceed. "Me too," he said. "We could share one." He glanced at Randa then added, "What are you drinking?"

"Ouzo."

Lucas blinked. Interesting. "Make one half of our platter ouzomezédhes," he told the waiter.

"And to drink, sir?"

Lucas knew this waiter, the lad Silver; he suppressed a grin on hearing the appellation 'sir'. "Ouzo for me too," he replied.

Lucas sat back, feigning relaxation. By ordering ouzo he had sent a signal to Randa that the scent and taste jousting to come would be on neutral territory – they would both stink of anise.

"A couple who eat garlic don't smell it on each other's breath," Randa observed.

"Indeed," Lucas replied.

They ate sparingly of the ouzomezédhes when the food arrived. These were indeed only appetizers, the negotiation yet to begin.

Twenty minutes later Silver approached the table. "Are you ready to order, sir, madam?"

Randa nodded, the neoprene menu held between two fingers, like a cigarette. "I'll have the briam," she said, "but go light on the onions."

Lucas nodded again. Briam consisted of summer vegetables – sliced potatoes and zucchini in olive oil, also eggplant, tomatoes, onions, and many aromatic herbs. And it was a vegetarian dish. Along with almost everyone in London, Randa was vegetarian, eschewing meat-eating because of the economic conditions caused by the decline of the Western world.

"I'll have the domatokeftedes," he said. A Status Quo speciality: tomato fritters with mint, fried in olive oil and served with fava paste.

They waited in silence for their meals to arrive. The strains of saz music wafted out of concealed speakers, Turkish imported nonsense that his mother insisted on since consorting with her Istanbul-born lover. Lucas rapped his fingernails together and noticed that his heart was beating faster.

So the negotiation began. From her briefcase Randa took tiny glass bottles of Palestinian artificial spice, which she used to season her food before eating it. These spices augmented the pre-programmed scents of her breath, carrying secret knowledge to Lucas through the machinery of the biochemical format; engineered molecules holding thoughts, arguments, positions, the shared language of patchwork London, that miasma of the planet, where every culture, every race, every locality was represented. This was indeed a London estranged forever from the electronic world, which in its antiseptic e-mundanity was no place for human communication.

Palestinian life had always revolved around food; a time to spend with the family, or socialising, just being human. No wonder Jerusalem had been the first city to come to London after the Lebanese Bomb.

And Lucas learned much from Randa's breath.

The primary responsibility for the Church of the Holy Sepulchre lay with the Greek Orthodox Church, which, under the status quo, could not alter any aspect of commonly held territories in and around that building – at least, not without agreement from all the other communities of Jerusalem with an interest in the place. But now the Palestinian Christians were agitating. They wanted control of the building entrance.

Lucas quailed. In 1192CE no less a man than Saladin gave responsibility for that entrance to a Muslim family, the Joudeh Al-Goudia. This family was entrusted with the keys, remaining custodians to the present day. They held the keys right now, high up in their Tottenham Court Road eyrie.

At once Lucas realised he had to order dessert. Silver appeared. "I'll have the loukoumades please," he told the waiter. Fried balls of dough drenched in honey and sprinkled with cinnamon.

Randa responded immediately. "For me… galaktoboureko." Custard baked between layers of phyllo pastry and soaked with lemon-scented honey syrup.

Lucas prepared his artificial spices. Once again the immense, complex scent-machinery of the biochemical format rose from steaming bowls into the air, infusing knowledge into Randa's brain. And she was a bitch: she smelled it all. She would take it all back to her side, the format ensuring that everything remained confidential, a secrecy orders of magnitude more secure than mere electronic encryption. This meal could have no eavesdroppers.

They drank ouzo as the night wore on. Further negotiation was minimal – few glass bottles emerging from their briefcases. Lucas remained shocked by the brazen Palestinian move. Why had they done this?

Randa remained ice cool, as a negotiator should. The intellectual game faded and Lucas felt his emotions roiling inside him as she prepared to depart. He always felt like this after the diplomatic joust. He loathed it. He loathed this stupid, artificial life. But what could he do? He was his father's son.

For a second time Zeid and Lucas studied the packet of

sweets in the upstairs room of the Status Quo.

"Why, Father?"

"Listen," Zeid replied, "there is something weird at the root of this Schism. You know about the ladder at the Church of the Holy Sepulchre?"

"What ladder?"

Zeid brought up a black-and-white holo from the room's computer tube. "On a window ledge above the church's entrance somebody put a wooden ladder – some time before 1852, it's thought. At that time the status quo defined the doors and the window ledge as common ground, so the ladder remains in position, unmoved to this day, because of the impossibility of coming to an agreement about it. Look, you can see it in this pre-computer photograph. Old engravings, too."

"But that's ridiculous. Arguing over a ladder."

"Don't you see? No, you don't, do you." Zeid shrugged. "You're still young. The Palestinian Christians have deliberately chosen an intractable problem as the basis for their Schism. They know this one can't be solved. They've come to us with the Schism because we're the leaders, the majority. We are the Greek Orthodox."

"But why have they come to us?"

"That's the crucial question. After centuries of squabbling, why make a culture-shattering Schism over a problem that can never be solved? None of the communities of the Church the Holy Sepulchre would ever agree to the Moslem family giving up custody of the keys to the entrance. Who would hold the keys after the Joudeh Al-Goudia family? It would start a war. Another war."

"I don't understand any of this," said Lucas.

"Nor do I. But the Palestinian ploy is related to those sweets, and to this newborn child, whoever that is."

Lucas stared at the packet. The brightly coloured wrapper spiralled red, blue and green up the tube, beneath it silver foil. "Perhaps Randa is pregnant."

Zeid shrugged. Pregnancy was exceptionally rare in London these days.

Lucas pondered. "What about Ghinwa's brother Amin?"

Zeid nodded. "He's their weakness. He held the sweets, he told us they were being passed over the diplomatic divide. He knows something Randa doesn't. We need to work on him."

"I could work on him, maybe?"

Zeid shook his head. "No. You'll be going to the Jameed restaurant tomorrow evening for supper, taking our response with you. Like tonight, you probably won't need to negotiate in full. But it will give you a chance to work on Ghinwa."

"Ghinwa…?"

"Yes. I have a feeling she is in on this ploy." He paused, sucked his teeth. "We're both diplomatic families, aren't we?"

The Jameed, six o'clock. The sun soft through biochemical street haze burnished orange; the noise of computer chatter, of boots on plastic pavements.

Lucas walked into the restaurant. It was a notional opposite to that of his own family, light where his was dim, narrow and long where his was circular, low ceilinged where his was high ceilinged. Randa met him at the entrance; Amin lurking behind the bar to one side, sipping from a Czech goblet full of creamy arak. There was no sign of Ghinwa, but as he smiled at Randa and walked into a glass-screened alcove he detected a few molecules of her skin's perfume, as if scenting a topographical fossil. She had stood beside the alcove less than five minutes ago, he knew.

The alcove commanded a view up the alley, which broadened like an urban delta to give a view of Baker Street. A slice of Jerusalem lay before him, including one wall of the Church of the Holy Sepulchre, further away a golden segment of the Dome on the Rock, its bulk concealed by blackwashed apartments.

He smiled again as Randa sat opposite him. In the Jameed he was the visitor, so: "A molecule of lemon..." He left the rest unsaid, on a whim.

She smiled. Lucas sighed. If only negotiation itself could be so pleasant. What was it about religion that made the smallest, most ridiculous thing a point of contest? Was it the five thousand year shadow of patriarchy, casting gloom over the human condition? Men generally? The burden of the intellect?

She replied, "A molecule of orange..."

She had offered him the seat with the view, leaving herself the seat with its back to the window. Quite a compliment. A ruse, though? Part of the Palestinian strategy? He could not mention the sweets because he knew nothing about Randa's connection with the family running this restaurant; unlike himself, she was unrelated to the owners. Not unusual, no, but perhaps significant.

"Are you ready to order?" she asked, as he placed his briefcase to his left.

"Yes thank you," he replied, taking the tubiform menu from the upright skewer on the table. He glanced at it, seeing his choice at once; sensing moments later a waitress at his side. "Taboulleh," he said. Pieces of parsley leaf, bulgur, diced tomatoes, cucumbers, all sautéed with lemon juice and vinegar.

"Fattoush," Randa said. Toasted bread pieces and parsley with chopped cucumbers, radishes, tomatoes and scallions, flavoured with sumac. Neutral choices: these were standard Levant salads.

They ate in silence as the music of an Afghan rebec floated through the air. The alcove was clean and tidy, with almost no scent of its own, though the soft cushions of the seats, being old, held the faintest fossils of persons who had sat on them before.

And then Lucas' nose caught a hint of Ghinwa. He turned around, peering into the restaurant but seeing only Amin and some customers. Yet she was close, she was here, as if part of the negotiation...

They devoured their starters, Randa talking about the rich seam of Afghan music she had discovered in a Covent Garden dive. Lucas smelled no stress on her breath – this was casual talk.

Twenty minutes later they ordered their main meals.

Lucas had prepared himself, but he glanced down at the menu just in case the Palestinians had made alterations at the last minute. But they had not. This meal being an early 'Asha he ordered a light mahashi: stuffed eggplants, baby pumpkins, potatoes, carrots and marrows alongside a variety of grape leaves, cabbage leaves and chard.

"I'll have the same," said Randa.

Lucas raised his eyebrows. An unusual gambit, suggesting that the information she had for him was subtle in the extreme – no variation in the carrier molecules, as there had been at the Status Quo. What was this game the Palestinians were playing?

When the meals arrived he took the Greek Orthodox glass vials from his briefcase and shook them over his food, eating with gusto. Biochemical information emerged from his mouth and his nostrils, skewed by the artificial spices, floating across the table into Randa's sensorium, where they were picked up by her nose, and by her other nose, the fabricated Jacobson's organ in the roof of her mouth designed to collect the heavier organic molecules.

Again: Ghinwa! For a moment his entire sensorium twinged, a split-second dizziness, and his heart raced a few beats; almost a carnal sensation, a warmth in his limbs, in his groin. He coughed delicately to conceal this emotional reaction.

Randa's breath carried nothing unusual, no hint of

stress. Was it possible that she was unable to recognise Ghinwa's skin: olfactory blindness? Lucas had heard of such a thing, but it was thought impossible to bring about, so complex were the new noses, so intricate the human brain. Was Amin's family testing perhaps a new olfactory shield?

He shuddered. He needed to keep his emotions under control. He was a negotiator.

A multi-level game was being played here. Very well. He had a few tricks of his own. "I don't want a dessert," he said. "I'm full already."

It was the height of cheek. A bluff, yes, which Randa could ignore. What would she do?

She stared at him. Her face blanched. She was shocked.

Lucas clicked his fingers at the waitress. "Gahwah sadah," he said.

Randa nodded once at the waitress. A minute later the girl returned carrying a silver tray on which lay two small white cups and a brass bodum. Pouring this bitter coffee was ceremonial; Randa, in company, would move clockwise among her guests, judging them by age and status, pouring coffee from the bodum. In Palestinian circles it was considered polite for guests to accept only three cups of coffee, ending their last cup by saying daymen, always, which actually meant may you always have the means to serve coffee.

Lucas saw none of this because Randa told the waitress to serve.

It was a blocking move to match his blocking move. At once Lucas realised that Randa was unaware of Ghinwa's input in the alcove. He had refused to accept Randa's half of the negotiation. If she could smell Ghinwa here in this most private of spaces, she would know there was a problem and would move accordingly. That she had not, that she had countered with an insult, showed she was but a tool of the Jameed's owners.

Lucas sipped his gahwah sadah. And his vision blurred.

The mucous membranes in his nose filled with blood and his heart rate increased; and for a moment, a moment so brief it was like a single frame in a video file, he saw himself from another's point of view: a handsome young man at a table; a sensation of desire; an emotion.

Randa was thinking, her mind distracted, looking elsewhere. Lucas took a couple of deep breaths, turning his head aside to breathe out for the sake of politeness.

Ghinwa, possibly Amin and Ghinwa, possibly the whole family at this restaurant, were orchestrating events. He knew. But why?

What had he just experienced?

Human consciousness was private – impossible to directly access another's thoughts, their mental visions, impossible to hear what their mind's ear heard when their inner monologue was spoken. Similarly, the biochemical immensity that was the smell and taste of the London air was private, reserved only for dogs and bitches, the inhabitants of the city, who could not directly communicate what they experienced in any way – this the beauty, the elegance of the biochemical format, whose complexity and utility compared with mere electronics was as a Leonardo painting to a child's sketch. And, just as important, whose security was impossible to crack for any entity not human. Organic chemistry versus maths: chemistry won every time.

Human beings could talk about their private experience – indirect communication. Similarly, negotiators could talk about their olfactory experiences, could glean meaning from artefacts of odour and pass that on to ordinary humans. Yet he had seen himself from somebody else's point of view just now.

Lucas knew that the Lebanese Bomb had led to a different humanity. He was a child of that creation, as were all who worked in London restaurants. He suspected now that the Palestinians had made a discovery. There was a meta-negotiation happening here, and he lay at its heart…

and perhaps Ghinwa did too.

He breathed out, softly, so that he could sense his own breath at the back of his nose. Her odour was there. She was inside him.

Lucas departed the Jameed and walked down the alley into Baker Street. The sparkle of hallucinations that was neon within biochemically enhanced fog, green algae light in banks of mist, fluorescence amidst dust, burst into his eyes, combining with olfactory, London-standard knowledge: map position, ambient temperature, traffic updates (solar vehicles only in London Central since peak oil). He paused at the street junction, orienting himself.

There stood Ghinwa in a doorway!

He ran over to her. She grabbed him and pressed her lips against his. For a few seconds he kept his mouth closed, aware of the consequences of tongues... but then the moment overpowered what little resistance he had. He felt the passion within her in many ways, through all of his senses.

The kiss went on and on and on – they breathed through their noses. Lucas felt he was eating her, consuming her, taking all the information in her saliva, tongue-to-tongue, allowing it to register in his mouth and nose, feeling it emerge, like a dawning realisation, in his mind. An almost infinite complexity of molecules passing from her mouth to his, comprising knowledge that they both knew because he was a dog and she was a bitch. Was this then the truth of her influence at the Jameed, that she was a honey trap?

She gasped and pulled back, her hips locked against his, pupils dilated, cheeks heightened red as blood capillaries expanded. "Do you sense me?" she asked.

Lucas wiped saliva from his lips and chin with his jacket sleeve. "Sense you?" he asked.

She nodded, grinning.

"Sense you?"

"You and me, we're something special together."

"What are you doing to me?" he asked.

She replied at once, "I do like you – you were right. And you like me. I can smell your pheromones Lucas, you want me. That's okay, I want to be wanted. You're a man and I'm a woman –"

"Wait, what's this got to do with the Palest –"

"Shhh!" She put a finger against his lips.

Irritated, he pulled back, let her go. Translucent mist swirled around them, so that for a moment she faded from his vision. He said, "You're trying to trick the Greek Orth –"

"Lucas! The bigger picture?"

"The what?"

"Aren't you frustrated by the lack of heart in negotiation?" she said. "I am. My people are too. We want to use patchwork London to make something better, so there aren't any divides any more, no splits –"

"No schisms?"

"Yes!"

"Then the Palestinian Schism is all smoke and mirrors?"

She grinned.

Then he had a thought. "Wait. Why are you telling me all this?" He took a few steps backwards. "Why isn't this coming to me through…"

"Through my saliva? Because we're not done yet. All this is incomplete. But tonight's test worked –"

"Test? You mean… that moment when I saw myself?"

She nodded.

Lucas, aware now of a conceptual grandeur behind her ordinary, ragged lust, realised that he stood at a crossroads. There was a decision to be made. Perhaps they had picked on him because they knew he was dissatisfied with the emotional sterility of negotiation. Perhaps they had targeted him because he was young. But oh, he longed for this woman. Was that maybe the point of the Schism?

"But how could I experience your private vision?" he asked.

"You didn't. Human mental experience is impossible to transmit except indirectly."

"Then…"

"The biochemical format isn't neutral. It's recorded the last thirty years of what human beings have done in this city. It's got attitude. But people like you and me, we have access to those records – private access to what is effectively a public entity. An exceptionally selective entity, of course. You didn't experience my private mentality, you experienced a representation of it stored in the Ocean."

"The Ocean?"

"It's what we call London's accumulated, self-organising biochemical database – supported by fifty million computers all in love with organic chemistry. We're members of an exclusive club, aren't we?"

"Is it like a brain?" Lucas asked, dreading the answer.

"It's like the brain of a bloodhound. It can't ever do the consciousness thing because there's only one of it. But, like a hound, it can sense, think, remember, and grow. It's got character now. It knows us all, like a hound knows its master."

Lucas took more steps backward. "You're reeling me in… you're trying to trick me!"

"No, Lucas! You must eat one of those sweets for this to work."

He stared at her. "But you tried to stop Amin giving them to me –"

"No! I just didn't want you to know I wanted you to have them. You'd have been too suspicious. Lucas, don't leave me, please!"

He ran away, stumbling down Baker Street. He knew too much; and she was inside him, like a parasitic molecule whose barbs he dare not pull out for fear of destroying himself. Like all good negotiators he never forgot a smell, a taste, he just couldn't. Neither his nose nor his brain would allow it.

He told his father nothing. He told his mother nothing. He saw in his family a mirror of fragmentary London Central, that place of attempted diplomacy, that hopeless, amateurish association of too-male, too-intellectual, too juvenile people. His mother – too damaged to care about her marriage, too indifferent to her husband's feelings to conceal her boyfriend. His father – of Palestinian origin, though welded to the Greek Orthodox Church by oath unbreakable – too obsessed with the nuances of thrust and counter thrust to care about the emotional life of his son. He sobbed. His father had pushed him into the field of negotiation. No, his father didn't care about Lucas, his father only cared about the quality of Lucas' intellect.

Damn this family!

And damn this church. Was there a god? He didn't know. But, more importantly, he didn't care.

There came a knock on his door. He said, "Yes?"

His father entered carrying a glass of orange juice. "Hello. You look like you could do with a pick-me-up."

Lucas took the glass and downed the drink. "Thanks."

"You haven't told us how it went at the Jameed."

"Pretty well. I'll tell you all later tonight. For now, I'm tired."

"Going to sleep?"

Lucas nodded. "For a while."

Zeid turned away.

"Father?"

"Yes?"

"How come a Palestinian is here, in this restaurant?"

He smiled. "I'm only a Palestinian genetically. Don't get hung up on my race."

"Do you think you might be the cause of this Schism?"

"It was the first thing I thought of. But no. Patchwork London is dispensing with race, with genetics. It's all about culture now. That's why I have hope for humanity, despite what we've done to the planet."

"The planet?"

"The ecosystem."

Lucas nodded. "Thank you, Father. You've really helped me, saying that."

"Saying… what?"

"Oh, about culture. I agree. Culture is everything. Attitude. Genes are redundant, except, I suppose, as a way of maintaining variety."

"Variety?"

"In the human gene pool."

Zeid smiled. "You're a clever lad. Well done. Have a nap now, and we'll see you later tonight."

But when Zeid was gone Lucas whispered, "No you won't."

Eight in the morning of the following day: Lucas at the remains of Marble Arch beneath the line of the faux-Himalayas. A beautiful location – he'd been here all night.

He asked Ghinwa, "What's this newborn baby?"

In reply she asked him, "What do you think an emotion is?"

"Well, I don't know. You mean, psychologically? Ask a psychologist."

"You are a psychologist, we all are if we're human. But I want to know what you think."

"I suppose," he murmured, "when you're upset, you cry. When you've lost somebody."

"That's one emotion. But what is it?"

"Surely somebody more clever than me must have come up with the answer."

"You'd be amazed how few people have bothered to consider it."

Lucas shrugged. He was not unsettled by the question, more intrigued; but it was a difficult one. After a pause for thought he said, "I'm not sure I could know. Imagine me on the edge of a waterfall cliff. If I was a brave man, I'd be excited, but if I was a coward I'd be afraid. They're both emotions."

Ghinwa nodded. "Both of those are emotions that can happen in the same circumstance."

"Yeah… So they depend on the experiencer, you're saying?"

"They're cognitive."

Now Lucas nodded. He felt a stirring of excitement inside his body. "Then emotions must have actual meaning."

Ghinwa said nothing.

"I never thought about them that way," he continued. "If they have meaning – and, of course, they appeared during the evolution of human beings, didn't they? – then there must be a very good reason for them. A survival reason."

Ghinwa nodded, then smiled and said, "Such as?"

"Well, I don't know… maybe they help us make judgements. If you meet a sabre toothed tiger, you get afraid, and you run away."

"They're value judgements," Ghinwa said. "And that's what I think. Certain experiences are basic to conscious human beings – the danger of death, the loss of people or things-"

"During our evolution we would have encountered those experiences often."

"Yes, we would. And the experiences began to engender various states of mind, which became universal states fundamental to the human condition. I think an emotion is the symbol of a state of mind, Lucas. Our minds have to have some method of communicating significant knowledge to ourselves, and to others. Without emotion, the mind would have no method of informing itself and others of the relative values of certain experiences. It's a strengthening and a validation of the mental model we all carry about in our heads. Do you see? By informing ourselves in this dynamic way, our mental model authenticates itself and allows other human beings to become aware of its state."

Lucas felt himself expanding, like an evanescent bubble, as if under the conceptual pressure of Ghinwa's idea. He said, "Do you think that's why emotions take over, why they always have a physical component?"

"Like tears? Yes, I do think that. It's because of the importance of the knowledge communicated. Lucas, I'm breathing fast out of the sheer excitement of telling you all this."

Lucas nodded, a grin on his face that mirrored her grin. "So some mechanism had to appear during our evolution that couldn't be missed, like a thought or a concept could be missed... a way of forcing the mind to become aware of such knowledge –"

"That mechanism had to appear, Lucas. It's why all emotions have an unmissable physical consequence. In its intensity and in its physical effects, emotion is impossible to ignore. I think emotion is a communicative reaction more profound than usual, not less. It's a channel of true connection between people and between people and the real world."

"A web of empirical knowledge flowing in all directions... An ocean."

"Ah," Ghinwa said. "An ocean."

He stared deep into her eyes. "Then... your Ocean?"

"It's not mine, nor even the Palestinians'. It belongs to humanity."

"Only dogs and bitches so far."

"Yes. But suppose, Lucas, suppose that now the Ocean exists we could make a brand new emotion never before seen in human beings. Do you think that might be possible?"

Lucas shook his head. "How would you genetically engineer its existence?"

"I don't think we'd need to. Objective observation isn't enough to bring understanding between different cultures during negotiation, since only surface features can be noticed. Emotion, with the involvement it entails, can bring knowledge more profound-"

"So that's why you chose me! You know I hate the sterility of negotiation."

"You're an emotional man." Ghinwa nodded. "Your father hasn't beaten all the feelings out of you yet. Do you have the sweets with you?"

Lucas took out the packet from his shirt pocket. "I've always disliked these religious arguments, that have to be negotiated away," he said. "That ladder in the Church of the Holy Sepulchre, unmoved for generations because men couldn't agree on a mutually beneficial plan."

"Emotion is the key to the new negotiation," Ghinwa told him. "But be warned. If you eat one of those sweets, you become like me. You won't be able to take sides any more. You'll be for everyone."

"How many others are there like you?"

"So far only my family. Randa is our neutral. We have other Lucases in other cultures, in other churches, but you were always my favourite. Honestly Lucas, I really do like you. I just didn't know about your feelings until that moment in the Jameed when you said you were lonely."

Lucas shrugged. "I don't know why I said that."

"Because it was the truth. I picked up on that. I'm a bitch."

"And the newborn...?"

"The newborn emotion will be one of compromise, of the perception of compromise in individuals. It will have a physical component that can't be avoided, so that the people experiencing the value and the importance of compromise don't miss it. Eat a sweet. Become like me."

Lucas looked into her eyes. "Ghinwa, are you entirely Palestinian?"

"Yes."

"But I'm Greek Orthodox. In theory... in practice, we shouldn't be able to compromise, no religion can admit that any other is correct –"

"Eat a sweet."

"What did you make them with?" he asked.

"Artificial spices regulating the experience of the new emotion in your mind. The Ocean will feel that emotion too, and then all the dogs and bitches in London. Isn't that amazing? So eat. Begin the transformation."

Still Lucas stalled. "Is Ghinwa your real name?"

"No, of course not! I chose song for a reason."

Lucas nodded. "You'll tell me your real name after –"

"After you eat the new idea."

And Lucas did eat. And as he looked again at Ghinwa – beautiful, happy, radiant Ghinwa – he felt a new sensation within his body, a kind of warmth in his chest that rose like soft magma into his throat, then made him breathe fast and deep... And as he breathed, as he felt that warmth, and as he pondered the importance of compromise, his mind turned on a previously invisible axis, to take a new position.

"I feel... amenable," he said.

Stink-Thinking

Frances Hardinge

And there it was, that familiar perfume. A little like fresh plums and custard, with a touch of clean, green, cut-grass outdoorsiness. The scent stopped me dead in my tracks on the front porch.

I could see nothing of her at first. My morning walk with Matt had taken me through a light shower, and sunstruck droplets still clustered on the stiff hair around my eyes, filling my vision with stars. Then the sun went in, and the dark question mark on top of the ceramic urn resolved itself into a familiar shape.

"Hello, stranger," said Lu Lin.

She was sitting on the urn, hunched forwards in her old fashion, feet drawn up neatly beneath her. While I was staring at her, Matt walked into the house and closed the door behind him.

Lu Lin was smaller than I remembered, and I was suddenly aware that her head would comfortably fit inside my mouth. And yet, standing in that unwearied gaze, I became a shambling youngster in an instant. Her great, blue eyes were luminous and bottomless as ever, and now they had a mesmeric expectancy.

I shook the rain out of my eyes, and with it the blithe, unthinking contentment that I had been enjoying for the last year. Lu Lin was back. If I wanted to talk to her, I needed to remember how to think in that dark, twisting fashion that came so naturally to her. And as soon as I started to think, of course, something occurred to me.

"You're dead," I said.

"Do you know your tongue was hanging out?" she retorted. "Disgusting." She stared intensely into my eyes without betraying the slightest expression, then leaned forwards precariously, laying her cheek against mine for a moment. "I really have missed you, Benjamin." I could feel her shaking a little. Perhaps her legs were trembling with the strain of balancing. "I was afraid you wouldn't come back." She straightened again, and her tail returned to its question mark.

"I've only been for a walk," Something was wrong. "Matt – he's shut me out, and he hasn't tied me up…"

"You know the really depressing thing? You're probably the most intelligent friend available." Lu Lin's contralto was as smooth and toneless as cream, but I sensed that this was not intended as a compliment. She dropped softly from her seat on the urn, paws thudding softly on the turf like raindrops. "You're not wearing a leash. What does that tell you?"

"It… fell off?"

"So you think Matt put it on when you went for a walk with him. Oh, Benjamin, *think*. I taught you to think, my sweet, didn't I?"

So she had. I believe at first I had thought she was my mother. I know I once tried to follow her onto the sofa back and balance along its length. I remember my fear of her strange moods and incomprehensible expectations, my desperate desire to win her approval, the torture of trying to follow the nocturnal swirls of her mind.

Only as I came of age had I realised that she was not my mother, but something fascinatingly and eternally other. When confronted by her slender, snaking form, I had found myself gripped by guilty, powerful urges, many involving chasing and trees. Lu Lin had seemed to sense my change, but had taken a wilful pleasure in provoking me, seizing every opportunity to flaunt her toothsome allure.

"*Think*. Can you remember this morning at all, before

your walk? You can't, can you? Let me explain. Matt didn't attach your leash this morning, because he couldn't see you. He thought he was going out alone."

I had an uneasy feeling that this was meant to reflect badly on Matt. I yawned and licked my nose, a nervous habit I have when I'm suppressing the urge to bite something.

"Oh, I'm not casting aspersions on your precious fellow. In fact, right now I'm the best friend he has in the world – excepting you, of course. But let's discuss this inside."

"I'm not allowed in when I'm wet and muddy," I pointed out quietly.

"Darling, all those rules are lovely in their way, but now is a good time to find out which ones you can break, and which ones you can't. And don't worry about the door. Just close your eyes and follow me."

I think I knew that all my choices rested on that one moment, that I could still return to my happy thoughtlessness. But along the other path stalked Lu Lin. Her every limb seemed as supple as a tongue, and moved as if tasting the air. Perhaps that blood-instinct that should have sent me chasing her to the high ground had been twisted out of shape, so that instead I felt compelled to follow her eternally. And perhaps that poisonous question mark of a tail had hooked deep into my soul, so that I too felt a need to ask questions. Even a terrier cannot be raised by a Siamese without ending up a little feline-minded.

I closed my eyes and followed her into the dark. Something brushed past my muzzle, my flanks and my tail like a cobweb. I opened my eyes, and I was standing in the hall.

"Go quietly here," said Lu Lin. "Gerbil district. I'll explain later."

The hall was darker than I expected. The lights were off, as they always were during the day, but the light from the window was blocked by a thousand tiny, tireless, winged bodies – flies, wasps, moths, a few blundering bees and a gangle of crane-flies. Occasionally a tiny body would tumble to the sill, spin giddily on its back, then find its feet again.

I flinched when a goldfish swam slowly past through the air, gills slack and eyes lugubrious.

"Poor thing. He's trying to circle his bowl, but he can't remember where it was." Lu Lin laughed softly.

"How long has there been a goldfish?"

"Oh, it was before your time. There *was* a goldfish… for a while." She narrowed her eyes so that the moonstones inside them glimmered. I smiled back, without knowing why. "Come, we need to get out of the hall. I think they've noticed us." There were sounds of activity in the under-stair darkness, and the scrabble of tiny claws on wood.

"But the gerbils…" I remembered a series of sad little lumps half-buried in sawdust. I recalled a hutch being scrubbed in ugly-smelling bubbles on the front lawn, and then taken away in a stranger's car.

"You're starting to understand, aren't you?" She looked at me dispassionately. "Poor darling. Let's go into the lounge."

Here too the windows were black with maddened flies. Feeling the soft, cream-coloured carpet underpaw, I remembered my wet coat and felt a frisson at the wrongness of my presence. And, yes, it was a frisson not unmixed with excitement.

Lu Lin leapt onto the arm of the vast, shabby sofa that stood before the fireplace, with a faint snick of claws catching in cloth. Tail erect, she inveigled her way through the cushions, here and there sinking almost chest deep in patchwork and satin.

I trotted around the sofa and found her lying at full stretch. Her apparent ability to triple her length at will always fascinated me. My tongue stuck in my throat as I noticed that she had reclined belly-uppermost, an almost unprecedented gesture of trust and affection. I was almost driven to do something rash, like licking her across the nose, but I restrained myself.

"Take a seat," she said. "No, silly boy, not down there, up here."

"I'm not allowed on the sofa."

"No one will ever know." The tip of her kinked tail often seemed to move with an independent will. Right now it was flicking to and fro, half-teasing, half impatient. "Look, Matt is in the most desperate danger and trouble, and I've just about made up my mind to tell you about it, but I won't breathe a word until you've joined me up here."

I was tortured by the image of Matt rapping me on the nose, his face patient but reproving. However, I gathered my will and with a swift kick of my back legs I was up. The sofa was soft and shapeless, subsiding in unexpected ways beneath my weight. It smelt of Matt and spilt bolognese. And Her, of course. Lorraine.

The silken bulges of the cushions were cool against my nose, and I struggled to concentrate.

"Matt's in danger?"

"Mm? Oh. Yes." Lu Lin narrowed her eyes again, but this time not in a smile. "Do you remember the 'bad man bark' you sounded a few nights ago?"

"Yes – bad man in the garden. Bad man." I growled a little. "I scare him away."

"Oh, don't go doggy on me again. Try to focus. The bad man is a friend of Lorraine's. She and he have been making kittens. I know the smell, even if Matt doesn't." I did not really understand what she meant, but I kept listening. "Anyway, you bad-man-barked four nights in a row, when Lorraine's friend was coming to help her make kittens, so she put something in your food. Something to make you dead."

Dead.

My mind squirmed away from the word. I felt my muzzle pucker, trembling between a growl and a whine. A bitter taste came into my mouth, and with it a memory of eating at Lorraine's feet while she tousled the fur of my neck.

I felt a sick lurch, a sinking sensation. Like the treacherous cushions, my happy, little world was giving way under my feet.

"I'm sorry, my sugar mouse," Lu Lin said quietly. Perhaps she really was. "But you need to *listen*. Because now she's putting it in Matt's food. She's trying to make *him* dead."

That was something I could hold onto. Something I could sink my teeth into and grip.

Matt was in danger. That was all that mattered.

Matt was in danger, and... it sounded as though I was allowed to hate Lorraine at last.

"But you..." I struggled to think clearly. "You were always Lorraine's *friend*. Me with Matt, you with Lorraine. Why... why are you changing sides?"

"I have my reason. In fact, you're sitting on it." Lu Lin extended a single claw and plucked at the worn corduroy of the sofa arm. "I've known Lorraine a long time, and recently she's been laying strips of cloth against everything."

I stared at her.

"It means that she's going to change everything," Lu Lin explained. "Old things go out, new things come in. She wants to make the whole house her territory, and smell of *clean*." She looked up and dazzled me with those luminous eyes. "Oh yes, she had a comfortable lap and was good at stroking, but she wants to get rid of my sofa, so she has to go."

I thought this over, with great care.

"Do I bite her?"

"Oh, you're sweet to offer, but it wouldn't do any good. I've experimented, and she doesn't notice, though it does seem to make her nervous. But... if I put my mind to it, I can move *things*." She kneaded idly at one patchwork cushion. "Providing I used to toy with them when I was alive, that is.

"Now, listen, Benjamin. Lorraine keeps her Bottle of Bad Death in her handbag. You used to fetch that bag for her, didn't you? That means you can still move it. I need you to take it from Lorraine's room while she's sleeping, and spill it over the floor where Matt will find it when he gets up. Simple enough?

"You will have to be careful, though. The hallway and the stairs are gerbil districts. Oh, most of the gerbils just hover in the air where their hutch used to stand, and quiver a lot. But the others... have started taking orders from the radiator in the utility room."

I shook my ears a little, but the words they had heard remained the same.

"Is it a... *ghost* radiator?" I asked.

"No." Lu Lin narrowed her eyes. "Radiators don't have ghosts. But for some reason *that* radiator is unusually talkative. I don't know why – the gerbils won't let me get close.

"I would get Lorraine's bag myself, but I was never allowed to touch it. She didn't trust me, you see." Lu Lin smiled at me with two blinding azure slits, then contracted herself into her usual dimensions and sat up. She laid one paw in play-fight fashion against my muzzle, the very tips of her claws resting on the skin under the fur. "You will do this for me, won't you?"

I spent the next hour barking at cars to clear my head.

Dusk crept in like a dingy stray. When Matt came to the front door in his stripes to put out the garbage, I crouched in the hall like a criminal and watched him.

Matt smelt ill. His hands shook when he knotted the garbage bags. Only when he had disappeared back upstairs did I dare to move.

A gerbil hutch had once stood on the high table in the

hall, and this location was now a centre of tremulous, neurotic activity. Tiny, rounded, frantic forms scrambled over one another in mid-air, confined between floors and walls which could no longer be seen. One of them ran his legs to a blur in an invisible wheel.

I passed their hutch without sparing them a glance, and approached the stairs. Already I was noticing traces of the other gerbils, the rogue element. Lu Lin was right. They had changed.

Their scent was bold and fearless. Tiny, proud tooth-graffiti had been nibbled into the bannister base. From the shadows I heard the faint, grating sound of rodent snickering.

Then I saw one of them, sitting in the middle of the fourth step, chewing on something that smelt like damp plaster. He watched me approach without flinching or blinking. When I came within lunge-and-snap range of him, however, he gave a high, sustained squeak. It was echoed by identical squeaks from the stairway and hall behind me.

The first attack took me in the tail before I knew what was happening. Next moment my plaster-chewing friend had leapt for my ear, and a couple of his hutchmates had me by the hindleg. From the hallway more were coming, a legion of little claws fretting at worn wood and carpet.

I sprang, twisting in mid-air, and felt the gerbil front-runners lose their tooth-hold on my fur and flesh. I leapt and scrambled my way up the stairs, blundering headlong into the murk of the landing.

Lorraine's door was always slightly ajar at night. I could just make out her door crack in the murk, a narrow slit of denser darkness.

The gerbils had not followed me. As I panted, however, I realised that I was not alone on the landing. From the shadows ahead came a thick, breathy, liquid sound, like somebody trying to drink from a hosepipe.

"No animals." It was a slathering splutter of a voice.

"No animals allowed upstairs."

"Listen, I don't want any trouble." I took a couple of shaky steps towards Lorraine's room, towards the voice.

There was a muffled scamper-thunder, and then a column of pale fur burst from the darkness and struck me in the chest. The impact rolled me onto my back, and then I struggling under the weight of a shapeless roll of carpet that seemed to have no head at all, just a neck with teeth. Sensing the precipice of the stairway at my back, I struggled free, and stared into a flattened face with doleful, insane, bulging black eyes.

"But *you're* an animal!" My nose was filled with the scent of another dog. Angry dog, sick angry dog.

The Peke gave a thin, mad, "Yi! Yi! Yi!" of rage, and rammed me again. I fell backwards into space, then felt stair after stair bite me in the spine and flanks as I tumbled. I hit the hallway floor with a force that knocked the senses from me. For a long time I lay stunned and motionless.

There was a dark and delicate whorl painted on the banister. It reminded me of Lu Lin. I watched it until I could almost imagine a kink in it, and a playfully twitching tip. At long last something in my own mind began to twitch and stir, and I started to think. I started to think the Lu Lin way.

The little plaster chewer was back at his post when I approached the stairs again.

"Hey, you." I said.

He stopped chewing.

"Not going to run away, are you?"

He started chewing again, but more slowly.

"You off your patch, doggy," he chittered after a moment. "Not welcome. You looking for trouble?"

"No, I'm looking for answers," I said, quietly. "Why don't you take me to talk to the radiator?"

Once the radiator would have gleamed, creamy sleek. Now

grey-furred cobwebs looped along the pipes, and a smudged hand-print on the paintwork had been commemorated in grime.

As I drew closer, my nose twitched. Behind the smell of dust and the cold scent of water slowly working its will upon wood and plaster, I detected something else - the fatty, fulsome smell of singed fur.

"Leave us." The radiator's rasping voice had a slight metallic echo. My gerbil entourage obediently melted into the shadows.

"Sir." I decided to direct my remarks at a central grease spot that looked a bit like an eye. "I understand that you and your organisation control the hall and stairway. I need free passage so I can reach the landing."

"Why, may I ask? For the pleasure of having your ears torn off by the Peke Pompadour?"

"Next time I'll beat him."

There was a pause.

"Draw closer," it said. "I want to see you."

I approached slowly, watching the wide, white surface for any sign of treacherous intent.

"No, to the side. Come, put your head against the wall."

Somewhat perplexed, I obeyed, pulling my ears back, and sliding the end of my muzzle into the gap between wall and radiator. It smelt like a bonfire after rain.

"Good," said a dark blot that crouched among the pipes. "Now, do not attempt anything irrational or aggressive. One squeak from me and my young friends will run in and tear you apart."

The speaker was about the size of a grapefruit, and the colour of under-bed tumble-fluff. Through a faint, sickly pall of smoke I made out a grey-furred face riddled with deep wrinkles and grooves.

"I must apologise for receiving you in this murky environment," said the Chinchilla. "I have... an aversion to light and open spaces."

"Are you stuck?" I had noticed that the Chinchilla's furred bulk seemed to nestle a little too snugly between the metal plate of the radiator and the slender pipe that ran along its base. There was a chill silence.

"I am quite content with my location. I will confess that, once upon a time, shortly after I had abandoned my hutch in search of a darker and more private abode, I did find myself incapacitated by the dimensions of this aperture. Its extremities of temperature were also... inconvenient. Now that I have adapted, however, I find it perfectly agreeable."

I wriggled my muzzle in a little further.

"I can try to get you out of there if you like."

"No need!" the Chincilla retorted sharply. "I have everything I require here. No light to offend my senses, no prying eyes, no gargantuan distractions. My young friends are my eyes and ears, and furthermore allow me to indulge at last my abiding love of strategy, something I do not expect you to understand. Every day I map a little more of this house in my mind's eye, and plan its conquest." The Chinchilla raised one tiny, grey talon before his face and wheezed out a lungful of smoke, then peered at me with coal-chip eyes. "So, how do you propose to best the Peke Pompadour?"

"By persuading you and your friends to help me."

"Ah." The Chinchilla laughed. "No doubt there is some excellent reason why we should do so?"

"Matt is in danger, and I need to carry a handbag down the stairs to save him."

"The heavy-treading male?" The Chinchilla's tone was cold. "He sometimes scrapes the mud off his boots against the radiator tap."

"If he dies, Lorraine will own the house. She will want to change and clean everything - including your radiator."

"Humans cannot see radiators," the Chinchilla

pronounced with confidence. "I have made a study of the subject. They never clean them."

"So... your 'young friends' are afraid of the Peke?" I felt as if my stumpy tail might be snaking like that of Lu Lin. "Then how do they get past him to spy out the upstairs for you?" I saw a flicker of discomfort cross my host's small, ravaged countenance. "I don't think they've even *seen* them. None of your people can get past the Peke, can they?

"But *I've* seen some of the upstairs rooms. If you help me, I'll tell you all about the bathroom, both bedrooms and anything new I see while I'm up there."

The little pouches under the Chinchilla's nose quivered as the tiny hands played lovingly along his whiskers.

"What if you burn out before you report back?" he asked sharply.

"Burn... out?"

"Moving things expends your energy, your essence. Dragging a handbag all the way down the landing could burn you out like a candle. You must tell me about the rooms now, just in case you do not return."

"One bedroom now. The other bedroom and the bathroom when I get back safely."

Another flame-crackle of a laugh, this time in assent.

Two stairs down from the top, I belly-hugged the stair-carpet and listened. On either side bristled an elite squad of gerbils, noses a-quiver. From the landing above, we could hear the irregular, soupy sound of breathing.

One twitch of the eyebrows as a signal to the gerbils, and then I took the last two steps at a bound.

This time the landing was not entirely dark. A bar of light spilt from Lorraine's doorway, kissing the carpet crimson. It gilded the fur of the Peke, and sparked in his maddened eyes.

"Bad animal," said the Peke. Black tears had worn little channels downwards from his nostrils and the corners of his eyes, as if he were truly saddened by my trespass. Then he howled like a hoover-blockage and charged.

This time I raced to meet him, taking the malevolent mop head on. He had weight and size on his side, but I had surprise. We rolled and hit the wall, a ball of fur and snarl.

Suddenly he pulled back and snapped at the air. His flattened head twisted this way and that, trying to fling loose the rodent forms which clung to his soft, shapeless ears. Others clung like rounded, brown burrs to tail and fetlock, collar and underbelly.

Seizing my moment, I leapt to my paws. I raced for Lorraine's door, and squeezed hastily through. The counterpane fringe tickled me as I dived under her bed, slinking myself flat against the carpet.

Things were not as Lu Lin had predicted. The handbag was not under the bed, and Lorraine was not asleep.

I watched Lorraine's feet walk past with their nails of pink metal. The door gently closed, leaving an arc of ruffled carpet behind it. Above me the mattress bulged and creaked, and the feet disappeared upwards.

When I crept out, Lorraine was stretched out on the bed in her shimmer-with-sleeves. She was box-talking very quietly, and she was twisting a long strand of her fur around her finger. Her voice made the same breathy, stealthy sort of sound as the door brushing across the carpet. It was a sound you could feel. To me it felt like being stroked wrong.

While she talked, she turned a little bottle around in her fingers. It was a cylinder with a cream-coloured cap, and a grubby label on the front. As I watched, she spilled four little white balls out of it into her palm, and put the empty bottle back into the handbag beside her.

My teeth tingled as I watched her lower the bag to the floor, and tuck it under the bed. I licked my nose, itching to snap at her fingers, but restrained myself because Lu Lin had said that might make Lorraine nervous. Instead I held still while Lorraine walked to the door, opened it again and slipped out.

I hooked my lower jaw under the slender straps of the handbag, with the deftness of long practice. This time, however, they might as well have been steel chains. My teeth could barely dent the soft plastic, and my jaw ached with the effort of lifting them. I heaved, paws scuffling for purchase on the carpet. The bag barely shifted.

Outside, I could hear Lorraine padding along the landing, and Matt's door creaking open. I could hear Lorraine using her ruffled carpet voice. Matt answered in his kind voice, his hello-there-and-ruffle-the-tummy-coat voice. He often used that voice with Lorraine.

Then I heard Matt's door shut. Lorraine's steps creaked downstairs. There followed the sound of the kitchen door singing open, and a clatter of pans. For a moment I felt only relief. Lorraine was out of the way, and would not see her bag inching along the floor.

Then my fur brindled as I understood what Lorraine was doing down in the kitchen. She was preparing their bowls - *Matt's* bowl. And she had taken with her four little white balls from the Bottle of Bad Death.

Desperate, I hauled, tugged and struggled with the straps. I was dragging a bungalow. My teeth were about to pop from my head. A roaring filled my ears, and I barely heard the slithering rasps as the bag yielded inch by painful inch.

Only when my tail struck against the door frame did I realise how far I had come. I shuffled my way backwards through the door, still dragging the bag. My legs were shaking now, puppy-weak. And as I tottered, almost slumping, the Peke hit me again like a furry train.

I nearly let go of the bag, but I did not. Some remnant of will kept my jaws clamped around the straps.

My strength was exhausted. The Peke was still in fighting form. But perhaps even that could be turned to account.

I staggered to my feet, offering a tempting, undefended flank, and he lunged for it, his momentum carrying us along the carpet. Again and again I managed to stand, always presenting a side-on target to be charged by the Peke. Again and again I let him bruise, buffet and roll me, always in the direction of the stairs.

"Bad animal," slavered the Peke, with the voice like eggs in a blender. He had me pinned against the banister, and there was nowhere left to roll. "Bad animal." The gerbil hanging from his eyebrow did nothing to increase the sanity of his appearance.

Then he faltered, jaw opening and shutting, rodent-beleaguered ears shifting nervously. Both of us heard a series of ascending creaks on the stairs.

Gerbils sprang out of Lorraine's path as she climbed, a bowl of steaming red on the tray in her hands. The red smelt of tang, and summer, and… and the strange bitterness of my last meal at Lorraine's feet.

The Peke sat back onto his haunches and made himself into a Toby jug of greeting, wiping his front feet through the air in front of his nose. Seeing him distracted, I lunged for the stairs with my last scrap of strength, the bag straps still clamped between my teeth.

I reached the top step at the same time as Lorraine. I felt my nose touch against well-washed person-skin, its texture somewhere between rubber and rose petal. Then the bag's leathery weight struck Lorraine's ankles, and one of her feet hooked in an unexpected strap.

There was a squawk from above me, and soup rained against the wall. Lorraine pitched forwards and landed with a crash, coming within inches of crushing me.

I lay helpless on the top step, panting for the breath I did not have and did not need, while Matt ran out to help Lorraine. Dimly I watched as he put his arms around her and helped her sit up, all the while using his hello-there-and-ruffle-the-tummy-coat voice. She sat rubbing at her leg, her shimmer gathered in ripples around her. Matt tutted over her spilt handbag, and picked up her shines and bobbles for her.

Then he stopped with inches of me, paused and frowned. Before darkness washed me away I saw him pick up a little cylindrical bottle with a cream-coloured cap, and stare at the label.

"I thought I'd find you here."

Lu Lin looked up from her urn-top meditation, and to her credit hid her surprise well.

"Benjamin!" She closed her eyes into the most entrancing sky-needles of welcome. "You are just the hero I thought you were."

"When were you going to tell me, Lu Lin, or were you hoping it would never come up? When were you going to tell me about the burnout?"

Lu Lin yawned. With half of my mind I was fascinated by how beautifully she sleeked her ears when she yawned, narrowing her face to a point, and the way her tongue curled like a rose petal. With the other half of my mind I knew that this was a trick she used when she needed a moment to think.

"I don't know what you mean." A beautiful level contralto. Sweet as summer plums. Smooth as custard.

"This was never about a single sofa, was it?" I asked. "It was a territory matter all right, though. Up until now, you've had the garden, and most of the downstairs. That would never be enough for you, though, would it? Not while there were beds upstairs, and all those perfumed bottles on the bathroom windowsill begging to be nudged into the bath. But the little rodents that used to be so scared of you had taken the hall and stairs, and some crazy old veteran ruled the landing."

Lu Lin smoothed her dark, grey gloves and said nothing.

"Was I supposed to come back at all, Lu Lin?" I demanded. "Or was I just supposed to eat my way through the gerbils, maim the Peke so you could finish him off later, then rain on Lorraine's parade before I burned out and left you with the house to yourself?"

She stopped grooming and regarded me steadily. A tiny, pink petal-tip of her tongue was still protruding, forgotten.

"I think I always hoped you would come back, and I am doubly glad now." There was no shame in Lu Lin's voice, no remorse. "I always hoped that some day I might look at you and see the eyes of a cat smiling back at me." She rose and stretched herself into a croquet hoop, pulling the pale sheath back from each precise translucent claw. "You and I, my darling, must have a long talk. You cannot imagine the plans I have for us, the ways we might spend our eternity…"

I watched her settle, mesmerised by her tail as it wound itself around her delicate feet. I ran my tongue over my nose.

"If you want me," I said quietly. "I'll be in the lounge, drooling on Matt's knee."

A Winter Bewitchment

Storm Constantine

Areta, the countess of Graserve, sat upon her morning terrace; the breakfast things had been cleared away. A clean perfume of star pine and doebloom wafted down from the hills behind the villa, warmed by the late summer air. The countess sat at a table of iron, forged carefully to appear delicate, which was covered in packages of letters and other papers. She wore a saffron morning robe and her luxuriant moss-blonde hair, thinly streaked with silver strands, was bound up on her head in a tousled pile. She was frowning a little. Her graceful left hand rested upon a stack of letters on her knee; these had been bound with a faded red ribbon, which now lay about them in a tangle. The lady's companion, a young, dark-skinned woman named Mimosa, sat on a stool beside her, helping to sort out the papers. The countess made a small sound.

"What is it, my lady?" Mimosa asked.

The countess smiled ruefully, her mouth turning down at the corners. "Ah well, I was only thinking." She tapped the letters. "Some of these are from my husband when we first met. He knew poetry then, of course." She laughed tightly. Her free hand indicated the letters on the table. "Some are from other men, dated both before and after the day of my marriage. Now they are no more than fading ink upon paper. I think I must burn them all."

The young companion stirred. She was from the far south, her dark skin tinted a curious shade of green that was so subtle you might think you imagined it, or it was a caprice of the light. "They are more than paper, my lady."

The countess smiled down at her companion, rested her right hand upon the unruly tumble of inky curls that seemed to burst from Mimosa's dark green head scarf. "I have no man to say sweet words of love to me. I have no man eagerly awaiting clandestine meetings, his heart full of poetry and beating fast in his hunger. I have no man to make exquisite love to me; I only have men who want sex, which is meaningless." She tapped the letters again and then shuffled them into a neater pile with both hands. "That is what I mean." She referred to her husband and her lover, both of whom had come to disappoint her. She thought upon how time had faded the splendour of first love, of excitement. All that was left was passionless domesticity in the marriage, and a kind of dull routine in the affair. She and her lover met for coffee, discussed books and plays, occasionally went to a hotel room, but there was no fire in their eyes, no fervour in their hearts. Hardly a point even for secrecy any more. Perhaps this was just an inevitable part of growing older.

The countess was quite sure she had said none of this aloud, yet Mimosa appeared to have heard every word. "Perhaps all this is true, but if you'll forgive my importunity, it is the love affairs that have aged. Your own ageing is irrelevant."

The countess raised her brows. "What are you saying?"

"You talk as if all is lost, but it is not."

"I'm not sure what is lost would be welcome back, in all truth."

Mimosa grinned. "If you could have any man in the city, who would it be?"

"Well, the obvious answer would be one, if not all, of the beautiful young things who strut about the stages of our world, or who paint, or who write books. There are many beautiful ones of those, aren't there?"

"There are," said Mimosa, but she too sounded unconvinced.

"But really..." The countess closed her eyes for a moment. "If it were to be any man, I would like it to be a man of character, of... power... perhaps someone of whom I might be slightly afraid. By that, I do not mean a bad or violent man, but something of a mystery."

"That too would be my choice," said Mimosa. "This is partly why my family sent me north, ostensibly to discover and learn about different cultures, but really to separate me from home. My choices were not universally approved among my people."

The countess laughed. "Were you sent away in disgrace?"

Mimosa sighed. "I wish that were the case. I simply kept a journal."

"Ah."

"It is no easy thing to have your dreams laid bare to the light of day, then mocked and criticised. I burned the journal as you are thinking of burning your letters, but if anyone is to destroy such precious memories it should *not* be the dreamer herself." For a moment Mimosa's face wore an expression of heartbreaking wistfulness, then she made a visible effort to pull herself together. "But that is not our subject on this beautiful morning. Come, my lady, think of the man you want."

"I think, dear Mimosa, there must be an archetypal man, who is the ultimate desire of all intelligent women. We could list all his traits, but is there such a man within the city?"

Both women were silent for a few moments, then: "Zachary Wilde," said Mimosa.

The countess considered. "He is handsome, true, rich beyond imagination, and overlord – for there is no other word – of one of the most successful businesses of our time. But he is also *very* married, and happy with it, by all accounts. His public image is of the contented family man, always seen with dogs and children." She grimaced. "I fear he is beyond temptation."

"Show me a human being beyond temptation, and I will show you a changeling," Mimosa declared, a trifle bitterly.

"I don't want another affair," said the countess. "It's far too demanding. What would be preferable is admiration, some fluttering of the heart, some excitement... Perhaps no more than that."

The conversation was cut short by the arrival of the count on the terrace. He was a tall, lean man, who like his wife had aged well. He was still what was called 'darkly handsome', and no doubt desired by many women who didn't know him, but he had a tendency to obsess over petty things nowadays, and had also taken to whistling in a warbling way, or humming tunelessly, both of which the countess remembered her grandfather doing.

The count sat down, lifting a sheaf of papers from his chair. He seemed not to notice the contents of the table, but nodded at Mimosa. "How's your father, my dear?" he asked. This question emerged every time he saw Mimosa.

The countess sighed inwardly.

Mimosa inclined her head politely. "He is very well, thank you, my lord. In his last letter he enquired about your new horse."

"When you next write to him, tell him I will be sending him a shipment of vine seeds, which I believe grow very well in southern soil. They don't do badly here, but from what I've heard wine made from these vines when grown in the south is like a catsup of the gods. In fact..."

"Well, let's clear away these things," said the countess to Mimosa, gathering up the letters and papers strewn around her.

The count began to hum beneath his breath, staring out over the terrace at the perfect sea.

The Wildes had come from the ocean, the family and their

entourage arriving two centuries before on three stout ships. The Graservites had been puzzled why this obviously monied clan had decided to uproot themselves from their estates in the western land of Saravey and sail *en masse* to Graserve. They had brought cobblers and farriers with them, bakers, farmers, sock-menders, jewellers, perfumiers and doctors. In fact, the entourage could well have comprised the stock of a small town. Before bringing any of his tribe ashore, the patriarch of the Wildes, Jebariah Amos, had requested an audience with the mayor of the city. The meeting had been private, but afterwards the mayor had appeared convinced the Wildes, though numerous, would be a worthy addition to the population of Graserve. The reason given for the mass emigration was that the Wildes were uncomfortable with the politics of their native land, where wealth and success were frowned upon as being the fruits of demon worship. Saravey was notoriously puritan, but it seemed conditions were worsening. In comparison to the average Graservite, the Wildes were to a man and woman far more prim and conservative in outlook. Only the fact that Jebariah Amos requested permission to build an estate some miles from the city convinced the mayor their rather alien ways wouldn't upset any of the natives. And he'd made clear to Jebariah Amos that he would countenance no subtle attempts at religious conversion. The Wilde patriarch had agreed to this. Subtly, and miraculously without causing insult, he implied it was the wish of he and his wife to keep their people separate from the Graservites. It was the land that had called to them from the sea as they'd sailed the coast looking for a home, not the people of the city. The mayor approved a parcel of land for the Wildes and tax arrangements were made to mutual satisfaction.

The Wildes flourished, and over the centuries mingled more with the people of Graserve. They always retained a certain aloofness, but on the whole were absorbed into the populace. As in Saravey, they became immensely successful in business.

Such was the heritage of Zachary Wilde.

Mimosa and the countess walked that afternoon in the Raven Park that overlooked the hills behind the city rather than the sea. They fed the ravens, paused by the fish pond to watch the lightning glimmers beneath the smooth surface, and finally sat down upon Lady Miranda Terrace, where they purchased tea and saffron buns, and here observed other walkers who came to refresh themselves.

"Have you thought more upon our plan?" Mimosa enquired.

The countess turned her eyes to the girl. "What plan?"

"Of seducing Zachary Wilde."

The countess laughed. "Dear Mimosa, I thought that was a game. I don't have the energy to make it a reality, even if I could." She reached out with a cool hand and touched Mimosa's cheek. "You, my dear, would stand far more chance of such a victory than I."

"I don't think you realise how beautiful you are," said Mimosa.

The countess was flustered by the compliment, also a little unnerved. "Well..." she began, touching her throat.

"It's a plain truth," Mimosa continued, "and it saddens me to think you've lost sight of that."

"I've not lost sight of reality," the countess said. "You are kind to flatter me, but the truth remains I am not a frothing girl with all the attributes of youth. Men, on the whole, like women young."

"Nonsense," said Mimosa. "I dare you to say that to my grandmother, who even to this day has men dying for love of her."

"Perhaps maturity is viewed differently among your people."

"It is, but mainly is this not down to how you view it yourself?"

The countess considered. "I see the wisdom in your words. Even as a girl, I believed in what my mother told me: that I should *think* myself wondrous at every social event I attended." She sighed. "Somehow, over the years, that conviction slipped away, and now it is more difficult to put on the mask than it was."

"What if I could help you put on that mask once more?"

The countess narrowed her eyes at Mimosa, but she was smiling gently. "I think you have a streak of wickedness in you, my dear."

"*That* is something I do not intend to let slip over the years," Mimosa said dryly. "Well, my lady?"

"Supposing... supposing you *could* do such a thing, how would it happen?"

"Slowly," Mimosa replied.

Zachary Wilde first saw her reflected in a tall silver vase. He was arrested by the sight of the slim figure that filled the gently swelling shape as if it had been painted there. He raised his eyes and saw a woman inspecting an array of candelabra on a merchandise table nearby. She wore a long dark coat cinched tightly at the waist and a wide, night-blue hat adorned with trailing black feathers. He could tell she wasn't young but on the other hand she appeared *ageless*.

This was the night of the grand opening of the new Wilde Emporium: a gargantuan indoor market that offered the produce of many distant lands; its food hall was a delight to all senses, oozing unidentifiable perfumes from dozens of unimaginable types of fruit and vegetable. In its cosmetics department were the same pigments and unguents that adorned the faultless faces of exotic foreign queens. Gowns and gentlemen's suits of curious cut were displayed on the clothing floor, if anyone could actually see them through the pressing throng of inquisitive customers.

Zachary Wilde was pleased with the launch, but then it

was no less than he expected. Now he was watching a woman in a vase, a somehow mysterious addition to his triumphant night. She did not appear to be reflected elsewhere, and yet a mass of receptacles of different shapes and sizes, fashioned from different materials, were arranged together – some with shining surfaces.

Wilde approached his customer. "Might I be of assistance, madam?"

The woman raised her head somewhat slowly from the item she was inspecting and regarded him. She did not appear to know who he was. She smiled. "I'm just looking, thank you."

He lifted a matte black, three-pronged candelabrum, turned it in his hands. "This was found in the catacombs of the city of Parnella."

"I am *not* anticipating a funeral." Her voice was low, humorous.

Wilde replaced the item on the table and laughed. "Yes, perhaps its origins should remain a secret."

Again she smiled. "I imagine your employer would prefer that."

"Well, if you need any help, please ask."

"I will."

Wilde was about to move away when an impulse seized him. He removed a calling card from the inner pocket of his suit. "Perhaps you would care to join us for a small reception once the emporium has closed. You would be most welcome." He offered the card.

The woman took the card and inspected it, holding it from her as if she was long-sighted. "Why is this?" she enquired. "I don't believe we've met before."

"I don't believe we have either, but my wife and I are inviting people who we feel will be... interesting."

The woman laughed. "I'm gratified to give this impression upon such short acquaintance."

He held out his hand. "Zachary Wilde," he said.

"Areta Winward," she replied, offering her own hand in return.

Countess Areta did not attend the Wilde reception but left the store discreetly once Zachary Wilde had moved on to talk to other customers. She felt rather dazed. Two days before, Mimosa had quietly informed her she must attend the launch of the emporium. The girl had been working on their project, she said, employing the ancient arts of her grandmother. The countess need do nothing but be present at the event. Zachary Wilde would notice her there, and in this way the scheme would begin. The countess must not pursue the acquaintance beyond the first meeting, whatever was offered to her.

Areta had to concede that all had gone as Mimosa had predicted, yet was there really magic at work here? Could it not be simple coincidence that Zachary Wilde had spoken to her? He was making his rounds of the floors after all, talking to everyone, hoping they would buy. He most likely told many of them they were 'interesting' and asked them to attend his reception. He could smell influence and money and no doubt scented it on her. This trait must be essential in his kind. And yet, the countess could not help but think of the fact that despite his groomed, affluent appearance, and the strong mien he wore that adorned all men of power, he had the most remarkable eyes. If anything, there was a deep sadness in them. This in itself was more attractive to an intelligent woman than gruff bravado, swaggering self-love or the blithe assumption than any woman would fall before him. These were not the beliefs of Zachary Wilde, she could tell. *Something* had influenced him. But no... It must have been coincidence.

As for Zachary Wilde, he found himself scanning the room throughout the sumptuous reception, seeking the tall, slender woman he had seen reflected in the vase. He remembered the exaggerated, attenuated shape of her. She had been somehow different to all he knew, gliding in a world that seemed removed from his. He found this extraordinary because he wasn't given to noticing women in that way. But he wasn't surprised she didn't appear. As time separated him from the meeting, she no longer seemed real.

Something can be made extraordinary by a single change to its being: a blue swan, a swan with human eyes, a swan with the voice of a woman. Or a small green cat. When Areta stepped out into the crisp autumnal air, with the blazing radiance of the Wilde Emporium behind her, she saw such an animal trotting up to her, tail held high, its great yellow eyes staring right at her.

No, she thought to herself. *No. Do not speak. Do not drive me from my mind.*

The way the animal was looking at her, she was truly afraid it might speak. How could she have such a notion? Before she'd left the villa, Mimosa had given her a calming elixir to drink, which must have affected her in an unexpected way. A cat could not be green, could it? Unless some rich woman had dyed her pet. People did that, didn't they? Areta turned away. She was rarely out alone, especially at night, and felt unsettled. The cat followed her, twined around her legs, mewing. When the countess glanced down, it raised itself to its hind legs, butted her coat with its head. She needed a carriage. This was a silly venture. Why had she agreed to go along with it? Briefly, she pressed both hands to her face. When she lowered them, the cat had vanished and a vehicle was approaching, which halted before her. She saw Mimosa inside it, beckoning, and then the door was open and she was stepping within. She lay half swooning on the plush upholstery as the carriage took her home.

The Emporium was dark and still, although occasionally the ponderous chandeliers would tinkle as if a breeze stirred their crystal drops and beads. Zachary Wilde had sent his family home. For now, he wanted to walk in his property, absorb the feeling of it, the sense of all those who had been there before. He was drawn inevitably to the second floor, where household accessories were displayed. Moonlight came in through the vast windows, conjuring gleams and stars in the cut glass, the polished surfaces, the silken drapes. Wilde's steps were almost silent upon the thick carpet. He smiled, thinking of how one day his ghost might haunt these halls and people would whisper of it. In that instant, the past, present and future seemed to converge and he felt disorientated. Was he already dead? Or was he visualising the emporium as he hoped to build it? No, he was walking within it, flesh and blood; his store existed and he was alive.

He came to the display of vases, which were gleaming in the moonlight. As he approached, he saw within the tall silver object that dominated the display the attenuated shape of a woman. Impossible. He glanced to the candelabra table, but no one was standing before it. Was this the answer? Her reflection had never been in the vase at all; it had been and *was* something else, a collection of objects around the room that mimicked the shape of a woman.

And yet, even as these thoughts formed in his mind, the woman reflected in the vase began to walk away, recede into the swollen image of the store. She rippled like ink until she was no more than a distant dark thread.

Wilde continued to stare at the vase without blinking for several long seconds. Was he going mad or simply overtired? He worked too long and too hard and perhaps this incredible *vision* was a symptom of that.

Over the following weeks, Mimosa arranged for the countess to be present in places where Zachary Wilde might be. She must not speak to him at all, and if possible not even catch his eye. She must merely hover at the edge of his vision, then disappear. Carriages were placed carefully to expedite this. The countess must seem to be a part supernatural creature, appearing and disappearing like a phantom. Mimosa had requested from her grandmother a particular perfume that was made on the family estate by female servants, who were tied intimately to the grandmother through a lifetime of witcheries and schemes. The countess must adorn herself with this scent whenever in the presence of Zachary Wilde, for it would linger on the air, long after she had departed the scene, and make him think of her. The countess was disturbed the girl might have revealed everything to her grandmother, but Mimosa stressed this was not the case. She liked to wear that scent herself sometimes, so it was not unusual to ask for it. When the green crystal bottle arrived, astonishingly quickly, it held within it all the spicy nights of the south, a breath of heavy lilies, a touch of earth.

The countess began to enjoy her little excursions; a visit to a theatre, an open air concert, a charity event held by the Wildes. She realised that she often passed by people she knew but they never acknowledged her, as if she was invisible to them or somehow changed beyond recognition. She did not, however, attempt to speak to them, in case this shattered the magic. She was content to be the ghost, gliding among the people, taller than most. She did not know exactly what Mimosa was doing, for the girl never included her in any of the procedures she undertook. She had no idea if the plan was working.

Zachary Wilde became a haunted man. Surely it could not be possible that the woman he was beginning to see more and more often at public events wasn't real? And yet he could never get close to her; she was always some yards ahead of him. Then she wasn't there at all. She left behind a lingering scent that somehow transported him, made him think not only of her but fantastic landscapes, exotic creatures, magic. He felt she must have a message for him, or was important in some other way, but how? If he could not speak to her, he could never find out. He shrank from confiding in anyone else about these *visitations,* as he chose to think of them. People would think him mad or else put some prurient slant upon the situation, which would demean what he was experiencing, and anyway was far from the truth. He dreamed of her, and when he awoke, her scent was in his bedroom, eclipsing the scent worn by his wife who slept beside him. The woman had told him her name but now he couldn't remember it, only that it began with an A: Aria, Arianna, Ava? The information had slipped from his mind. He had men who did clandestine *tasks* for him sometimes, but he shrank from asking any of them to search for a tall woman whose name began with the letter A. He could visualise their bemused expressions vividly, and even if they were the sort of men who would not talk, they would *know.*

Often, Wilde went to his emporium at night, hoping to glimpse the woman's form in the silver vase, but it was never there again. He realised upon one of these starlit excursions that he must arrange another event, because she was sure to be there, and this time he would be as tricky as she was. He would be invisible in the crowd, creep up on her and take hold of her arm. He would root her in this world with him and then... then something could be said or done.

The year was fading fast. Wilde felt he had to act before it ended. He would host another charity event in two weeks' time, just as the first festival decorations began to appear in houses, streets and stores. He would hold the event at the Glass Fortress, a building popular for such occasions, in the sprawling Raven Park to the north of the city. He would invite everyone of importance: landowners, rich merchants, doctors, scholars, lawyers, artists, actors... anyone of note. Surely his fascinating ghost would not be able to resist such a sweetly-baited trap?

"I hope you are ready," Mimosa said to the countess, one morning at breakfast, "because very soon you must speak again to Zachary Wilde."

The countess froze in the act of buttering a piece of toast. Her husband had already left the table. "I'm not sure I want to."

Mimosa smiled. "I know how you enjoy teasing him, but you must speak to him."

The countess was assaulted for a moment by a hideous image of panting breath and grappling bodies, which seemed altogether gross and undignified. "Why?" she asked feebly.

Mimosa reached out to touch her arm. "You can have a secret companion, a man in love with you, who will travel with you to marvellous realms. The enchantment must gain strength. You may speak of love with your eyes, with the very images you create before you, and kisses need not venture beyond the eyes. Do you trust me?"

The countess stared hard at the girl. "I do," she said, "whether against my better judgement or not, I do."

"Good, for I love you as I love my grandmother, and she, as well as I, want wonders to be yours."

"You *have* written to her about this!"

"No."

"Then...?"

Mimosa smiled, and all the secrets of women were held in that smile.

"I see... Well, all right, if it must be so. But I have no idea what to say to him."

"Some things should remain unscripted," said Mimosa.

"But what about the restrictions you placed before, such as not agreeing to go anywhere with him, or even speak these last dozen times I've seen him?"

"When he makes a certain invitation to you, you must accept," Mimosa said. "You will know when this happens. It might not be the first invitation. You must let him catch up with and speak to you, and let him believe he has snared you himself, through his own wiles."

The Glass Fortress was beautiful, a radiant fairy-tale palace dusted with the lightest touch of fresh snow. As Countess Areta alighted from her carriage some distance from it, the flakes settled softly upon the shoulders of her coat and upon the wide brim of her hat – the same dark garments she had worn the first time she'd spoken to Zachary Wilde. She walked slowly to the gleaming edifice ahead of her, which through the light snow looked as if it were made of ice. A scrum of carriages jostled at the entrance, as guests wished to avoid the snow; when Areta entered the building, she was the only one touched by it.

A man in dark red livery offered a tray to her, on which stood tall glasses filled with sparkling wine. Areta took one and sipped from it. The Fortress was filled with people, too many of them. Voices were loud and sounded hysterical to her. Every other woman seemed to be dressed in bright, festive colours, while she was this dark, looming creature; long black feathers trailing from the crown of her head.

Areta walked around the edge of the room. She could not see Zachary Wilde amid the throng but then there were so many people, all pressed together. Still, at previous events she'd been able to spot him straight away. He wasn't tall, certainly not as tall as she was, but he stood out remarkably: a neat man, with a short tidy beard and just the slightest unruliness to his thick, dark hair, which came to his collar. Areta noticed his wife sitting on a plush couch against the far wall, surrounded by friends and accompanied by her eldest daughter. This woman must see Zachary Wilde every day; to her he might be a mundane entity, hardly noticed. They'd been married many years. Areta smiled a little to think that some predatory female might even think that about her own husband. How sad and grim that the familiarity of years erodes the initial wonder of first meetings. In fairy stories, the tales end often with marriage, the princess and her prince. As far as she knew, no one wrote stories about those same characters after twenty or more years had passed. What would there be to say, other than to write about routine and boredom or in lucky cases comfort and companionship? No, it would be the grandchildren of those fairy-tale princesses who would be having the adventures by then, woken with kisses, rescued from peril and carried before brave knights on white chargers with their gowns and hair trailing down.

What am I doing? Areta thought. *What is possibly to be gained from this other than a brief frisson like a firework lighting the sky, its marvels gone in seconds?* She sighed. Mimosa meant well, and clearly enjoyed this little game, perhaps more than Areta did herself. But the time had come to end it. Waiting longingly for a man to appear in a room was a feeling that should remain in memory, for there could be no fairy-tale, no marriage, but possibly a variety of disasters.

Areta put down her empty glass on a spindle-legged table and at that moment, someone took hold of her arm, very firmly. Alarmed, she turned at once and saw she had been apprehended by Zachary Wilde himself. He must have discovered her scheme somehow, learned her purpose. Perhaps she would be asked to leave.

"Forgive me," said Zachary Wilde. "I didn't mean to alarm you, but I would very much like to talk to you." He smiled in a boyish fashion. "You look so very fierce. Please. Just a few moments of your time."

"I... I don't mean to look fierce," Areta said, feeling far from that. "But everyone is looking at us, Mr Wilde. Perhaps you should let go of my arm."

"And if I do, you won't vanish?"

"I'll try not to." She smiled then. He hadn't learned her deceit, after all.

Wilde let go of her and for a moment appeared unsure

of what to say. People were so close and because of who he was, and the fact they did not know or recognise Areta, they were curious.

"Mr Wilde, you are on the brink of causing a scandal. What is it?"

He appeared to control himself. "This might sound uhinged, but you've become rather a mystery to me. Let me explain. I see you so often, at nearly every public event I attend, yet I do not know who you are or why you're here. You don't arrive or leave with any companions. No one talks to you, almost as if they can't see you. And yet – I am happy to say – you are not a ghost. Will you satisfy my curiosity?"

"People can see me now all too well," Areta said sweetly. "In fact soon the whole room will be gossiping about me."

"Must you always remain a mystery?"

"There's nothing mysterious about me. I visit public events because I like to get out of my house. I enjoy them. But while I like to mingle with people I don't necessarily want to talk to them. What's mysterious about that?"

Wilde pondered her words for a few seconds. "Yes, I can see that now it is *me* who is being the mysterious one. But there is..." He narrowed his eyes. "No, to say more would make me sound even more unhinged. I do apologise. But despite that, I would like to know you better. Would you care to meet my wife and family?" He gestured towards the far wall.

Areta glanced in this direction and noted that Mrs Wilde was not paying attention to her husband's conversation – yet. She wondered if this was the invitation she was supposed to accept, but he'd made no others yet. "That's kind of you, but... I was just about to go home. I'm sorry. I have guests later."

Wilde pulled a face of disappointment. "What a shame. Perhaps you would be free to meet me at the Café in my emporium tomorrow?"

All around Areta, the occupants of the room seemed to be slowing down. Arms rose and fell as if under water. Heads turned languidly, but away from her. Voices became a low murmur. But it was not yet the moment to comply; she was sure of it. "This sounds as if I'm making excuses, but really I can't meet you tomorrow. I have prior engagements."

Wilde grimaced, raked a hand through his hair. "I wouldn't blame you for refusing, excuses or not. The request was perhaps importunate. How about this? Every year, we hold a party at our home just before the Winter Festival. I would very much like you to attend. If you'd give me your address, I could ask my wife to send you an invitation." His hand went to his jacket pocket, presumably for writing implements.

After a pause of three heartbeats, Areta said, "Thank you, I would gladly attend."

Wilde relaxed as if in great relief. He grinned, again with that almost heart-breaking boyish air. "Your address?" He held a pencil, poised, over a small notebook. Around them, the cacophony of voices started up again and people moved swiftly.

"If you will indulge me, I'd rather not give you my address. Might I simply turn up, or will I need the invitation to pass your threshold?"

Wilde considered. "I can leave your name with the Welcomer at the door."

"Splendid."

Wilde sighed, rubbed his face. "This is going to sound extremely rude, but..."

"But what?"

"What is your name?"

Areta laughed. "Areta Winward. Perhaps you should write that down." She held out her hand to him. "And now, I really must go. Congratulations on a marvellous party, Mr

Wilde. I shall look forward to your Festival celebration."

He took her hand. "I haven't told you the date..."

She let her fingers lie cool, but not limp, in his own dry palm, resisting an impulse to squeeze him. "The whole city knows what the date will be. I doubt there's any risk of me missing it."

"The 18th, at 8 o'clock."

"Yes. I know."

She felt him watch her wind her way through the crowd to the entrance. Of course, she must not attend. And yet... She resisted the urge to glance over her shoulder.

"He has my name, Mimosa," said the countess, "and this time he wrote it down, so he won't forget. He might try to find out things about me." She had recently arrived home and Mimosa had been waiting for her in her dimly-lit boudoir. While the countess had yanked off her hat, pins and all, and thrown her coat onto a chair, she still wore her gloves and a vanity purse dangled from her left wrist.

"There will be more than one woman in Graserve named Areta," Mimosa said, "and the chance of him discovering the name of your great-grandmother's surname on your mother's side is remote."

The countess put her hands to her face. "Oh! I am unnerved."

"This is plain to see," said Mimosa. "You look like a girl – a very excited girl, I might add." She was sitting on the wide canopied bed with her legs drawn up, her arms clasping her knees.

"Now, stop it, you naughty minx!" the countess declared, making a vague slapping gesture in Mimosa's direction, but she was smiling widely. Then her hands flew to her face again. "Oh, what am I doing? This is madness, and also dangerous."

"Isn't that the attraction?"

The countess picked up a cushion from the chair and

threw it at the girl, who dodged. Then they were hurtling about the room, laughing, ultimately throwing themselves onto the bed, out of breath. "You are the first proper witch I have ever met," said the countess.

"Your mirror might disagree," said Mimosa.

That night, Zachary Wilde dreamed of Areta Winward. In the dream, he was walking through a garden that was rather complicated with winding paths and too many trees, and shadowy people strolling among them. The shadows did not interest him. He was pursuing Areta Winward down a narrow walk. She was wearing a cream-coloured summer dress, but did not carry a parasol as the other women did, nor wear a hat. *This must be her garden*, he thought and called out her name. She turned, put a finger to her lips and then gestured for him to come to her. He saw there was a fountain of stone fish beside her, which had created silvery rippling patterns on her skin.

"Come with me, Zachary," she said. "I would like you to see the real garden."

She held out her hand and he took it.

Areta led him between high hedges of boxwood and then they were in a maze, the hedges towering over them, closing in. The woman increased her pace and eventually they were running, along narrow pathways, round corners, again and again. He supposed she was taking him to the heart of the maze, which would be magical, but then they turned another corner and were beyond the hedges. A landscape of extraordinary wonder and beauty spread down before him, as if an enchanted carpet was being shaken and unrolled before his eyes. He stood hand in hand with Areta Winward gazing over this sparkling vista. A white city of spires and turrets and banners reared over a green lake. Beyond was the lilac smudge of high mountains. From where in Graserve could this be seen? Or was it merely an image conjured by the soft sunset light in the peach-coloured sky, the fire-edged wispy clouds, that made it all so lovely? "Incredible," he breathed. "What a view you have."

Areta's hair was loose about her shoulders now, and her feet were bare beneath the hem of her dress. He drank in the sight of her; her noble height, her sculpted patrician face, her long hands and feet, the wheaten-gold of her hair. He had never beheld a woman so stunning to the senses: a pagan priestess, a witch, an oracle. "This is my garden," she said, "and it extends forever. Fear cannot live her, nor madness, nor despair."

"This is a dream," Zachary Wilde said sadly.

"Yes," Areta said, "but it is ours, and it exists, here beyond the portals of the mundane world. Inner life can be rich beyond imagination. We need discover only how to meet here, to step beyond."

And with these words she transferred to him the kiss within her eyes, hardly more than the passing of a breeze and yet so potent. Then she was some distance off, down the hill before him, eventually dwindling to nothing. She had a small green cat by her side.

On the night of the party, the countess dressed in a clinging robe of white silk velvet that had an enormous hood trimmed with snowy marten fur. Over this she flung a white satin cloak that had no hood but which reached to the floor. Mimosa arranged her hair so that coils of it were wound upon her head, while other locks flowed down over her breast, carefully curled.

The countess felt removed from reality. Over the past weeks, she'd been living two lives, one in the mundane world, the other... the other somehow lost in a dream of impossibilities. She had dined with her husband and had enjoyed his company. She had met her lover twice and had laughed at his wit. But all the while she'd been thinking of Zachary Wilde. Mimosa had done something terrible to her and part of the countess yearned to undo it before anything else could happen. But at the same time, she could not act.

When Mimosa told her the carriage was waiting for her outside, the countess moved slowly out of her room, down the wide, sweeping staircase to the hallway of her home. Her husband was absent at some men's gathering; he would not be back until dawn. The snow was heavier now than on the night of the Glass Fortress party; it came down in flakes the size of florins.

The Wilde manse stood upon a hill, surrounded by farming land and forests. The house shone like a festival tree; every window blazed with golden light. As if in a trance, the countess stepped from her carriage, passed the stamping horses, and climbed the shallow white steps to the main entrance. Here, her name was a charm that allowed entrance, and she became this *other* woman.

"May I take your cloak, madam," murmured a girl in uniform and Areta surrendered this to her.

She was late, intentionally, so that that Zachary Wilde and his wife would not still be in the hall, greeting the first of the guests. Now, they would be mingling among all these people. Areta knew she did not have to concern herself with speaking to anyone. Unless Zachary anchored her physically, she would remain unnoticed here. Servants, however, were immune to this effect and offered her wine in an indigo glass, and a small dish of delicacies. Areta drank the wine and nibbled on a few of the delicacies before discreetly leaving the dish on a table. She wandered through the radiant salons, looking at all the people. At one time, she'd attended parties like this at least once a week; now they were strange territory to her, no longer compelling.

Presently, a young footman approached her and asked her to accompany him. Languidly, half dazed, Areta complied. She followed the boy through the blazing caves and tunnels of the house, past many doors flung wide, until they came to a region, at the top of several stairways, where all the doors were closed and there was neither light nor noise. They were in a corridor, lit by the moonlight that fell through a tall, arched window at the far side. Here, as far as Areta could see, was a dead end but the page opened a door to the right, which revealed a flight of descending stairs. Alone, Areta walked down them. The footman closed the door behind her.

She came to an oriel hallway, dominated by an immense stained glass window depicting stylised blooms and peacocks that was circular at the top with a rectangular pane beneath. Two curling flights of stairs led down, one opposite to where she stood, these eventually conjoining into a single flight that led to a bare, dark chamber beneath.

And here Zachary Wilde was waiting for her, sitting on a simple wooden chair, such as you'd find in a kitchen. He did not notice her at first, lost in his own thoughts. He seemed so sad. Was she causing this, bringing a kind of madness into his life? Did he wish he hadn't asked her here, wished desperately he'd never met her so he wouldn't have to feel like this? Resigning oneself to an arid life was one thing, invoking the flaming follies of youth was another.

She could turn now, glide back up the stairs, find her way out. She didn't need to subject them to this; the power was hers. But then he raised his head, and while the sadness remained in his eyes for several long seconds, this was presently replaced by joy. He stood up, held out his hands to her.

Zachary Wilde regarded this creature as she came to him; a snow goddess, an ice nymph, a sorceress of blizzards and storms. How could she possibly be real? Yet here she was. "I didn't think you'd come," he said. "I'm not sure anymore what is a dream and what is reality."

"I feel, Zachary, that this is both," Areta said, and took his hands in hers.

"I've realised I have somehow fallen in love with you,"

he said, "and yet I don't know you. What I love is hardly more than a ghost, or the woman I would like you to be. The fact that you are here..." He frowned, shook his head, gazed at her once more. "Do you feel anything of what I feel? Or are you really a delusion, a vision?" He laughed sadly. "Can you even answer that?"

"You don't have to worry you are going mad," said Areta gently. "I am real enough, and yet perhaps our meeting here like this is not. I think we are perhaps seeking something we have lost – the gardens of our youth. In each other's company, those gates hidden by ivy and cobwebs and years are somehow unlocked. Will you follow me?"

He nodded. "Yes."

He went after her out into the silent garden, over the snow-crusted lawn and then onto cold paved pathways. He followed her into the ice-mantled trees at the edge of his estate, and then into the winter fields beyond. White, winged creatures that were not birds flew across the gemmed sky, which looked as hard as frost. If he reached up, perhaps he could pluck the gems right from it. And still he followed her, across frozen rivers, through sleeping hamlets and into the foothills of white mountains. She ascended the snowy slopes with ease, never faltering, while now he was stumbling, the cold biting right into his bones; his shoes and trousers were sodden, his feet numb. But above him, in the mountains, he saw the soaring turrets of a marvellous citadel, golden lights gleaming from all its windows as if in welcome. Near, yet far. He was too weak in body to reach it, the icy frost too severe for his flesh. When he thought he must die of cold and exhaustion, he called to Areta to stop and wait, and she did.

"We have come too far," he said.

She smiled. "No, not far at all."

Then he turned to follow her gaze and saw the lawn of his house, with their prints in the snow – his shoes , the serpent trail of her hem – and beyond this the festive shine of his home. There were no mountains, no shining citadel. He fell to his knees, panting.

"When I first saw you tonight," said Areta, "I thought of turning back, for I have no wish to cause you pain. But then I knew how I could show you the truth. Do you see now?"

He shook his head.

She leaned over him, took his face in her hands. "What are the passions of youth but fantasies, idealised landscapes and blissful dreams? We can *be* this – in some precious moments. I don't know how to explain, nor truly understand it, but perhaps it is a gift we should not question."

He clasped her legs. "Is there not a danger we could vanish into that world? It seems..." His gaze shifted to the trees beyond the lawns. Snow had begun to fall again. "It seemed so real."

She stroked his hair, which was dappled with snowflakes. "We all know, Mr Wilde, that dreams – like this festival snow – do not last."

The countess arrived home in a tranquil yet thoughtful mood. As before, Mimosa was waiting for her in the boudoir. "Well?" she asked.

"A dream happened in reality," said the countess, slowly taking off her cloak, her gloves. "Zachary Wilde and I both saw this; it was quite real. I don't know how I took us there, but I told him I could do so again. Is this true or was I deceiving him?"

"You have the ability now," Mimosa said.

"Rather more than a mask."

"Yes. Rather more."

The countess pinned Mimosa with a stare. "I noticed you weren't there tonight. I saw no green cat."

Mimosa smiled and rose from the plump chair where she was sitting. "What makes you think the cat is me?"

The countess merely laughed.

"Did he declare his love for you?" Mimosa asked.

"I don't think he knows himself what he feels, other than bewitched." The countess frowned. "If he does indeed believe he loves me, it is not through my own doing, or the charm of my personality, is it?"

"You're not supposed to care about that," Mimosa said.

"I care about hurting people, stupid though that may be." The countess sat down in the chair Mimosa had vacated and rubbed a hand across her brow. "I know you meant the best for me, my dear, but I can't foresee anything good deriving from this deceit. I am in a superior position to him, having much freedom. He has a large family that demands his time, never mind the work he has to do. He has too much to lose."

"His wife and family can't follow him into a dream, especially when it isn't his own," Mimosa said, rather coldly. "And I don't believe you want it to stop. You would miss him, wouldn't you...?"

The countess held Mimosa's gaze for some moments, as a thread of realisation stitched through her mind. "What is this to you?"

Mimosa turned away.

The countess got to her feet. "There *is* some personal reason behind all this, isn't there?" She shook her head. "Have I been even more foolish than I thought?"

Mimosa wheeled around. "No, no, I want nothing evil for you, my lady. I care for you very much, but..."

"But?"

The girl took a deep breath. "There is more than one race whose people are in some sense refugees upon this continent. My family too once came from Saravey. We were... We were driven out."

The countess gripped Mimosa's shoulders, shook her slightly. "Mimosa, please tell me this isn't some personal vengeance you're enacting upon Zachary Wilde's people –

his *ancestors*, even."

Mimosa would not meet her eyes. "The Wildes were part of it, the cabal of men who stole our land, accused us of crimes we didn't commit."

The countess expelled a small groan. "You speak of 'we' and 'us', child, but whatever happened was hundreds of years ago, terrible though it might have been. Your family have lived and prospered in this land for centuries, as have the Wildes. If anything your father is richer and more powerful than Zachary Wilde. Can't you see that the past is not relevant to you now?" She held Mimosa close. "My dear child, don't let your young heart be corrupted by these bitter feelings. Please!"

Mimosa's voice was muffled, as her face was pressed against the countess' chest. "I never wished you harm, my lady. Haven't you enjoyed our story? It has brought you happiness, hasn't it?"

The countess held the girl at arm's length. "Yes, it has; a pleasant dream, but perhaps not for him. Wasn't that your design?"

"To ruffle his smug existence?" Mimosa smiled wanly. "A little maybe."

"A lot, I think!" The countess sighed. "Now this sport must cease." She kissed Mimosa's brow. "Go to your bed, my dear. We have much to plan for the festivities ahead."

Left alone, the countess allowed a few tears to fall, but only for a short while. After this, she dried her eyes and confronted herself in her mirror. She and her reflection smiled at one another. Then she went to bed.

On the festival day, after a late lunch, Zachary Wilde felt an urge to leave his family and the warmth of the house. He went out onto the terrace beyond the drawing-room. Even so close to his people he felt alone. He found waiting for him a black lioness, seated upright on the cold pink granite that had been swept of snow earlier by servants.

He stared at her and said, "Is this you, my heart?"

The lioness stirred, and as she rose to her four great paws, obsidian wings unfurled about her. The bright winter sun conjured shades of blue, purple and deepest green in the jetty feathers. She regarded him with snow-blue eyes, and as if dreaming he took a step towards her, with every intention of climbing onto her broad back.

But then it happened that his youngest grand-daughter came out onto the terrace, running and chattering, as a child will. In a moment the lioness spread her wings and then was in the air.

"What are you waving at, Grandpapa?" asked the child.

"A lioness with wings," he replied.

"I want to see her too." The child came to stand before him, leaned against his legs. "But where is she, where?"

"There, my dear." He pointed.

"Does she want us to go with her?"

"We can go with her if we want to."

"She's flying away."

"Yes, she is. This time." He lifted the girl in his arms and together they gazed at the already distant speck.

Andrew Hook

Apricot brushed a strand of brunette hair away from her right eye. It was a self-conscious movement, yet utterly natural; like a leaf falling from a tree. She stared forwards at the vacant chair behind the large oak desk, resisting the urge to look around the empty, windowless, office. She had been ushered into the room and told to wait until Mr Grantham was available. One of her legs was crossed over the other and she sat straight. She had a feeling there might be a recording device present and so she considered her posture as if Mr Grantham were already in the room. She wanted to keep it professional.

If there were a device, it might be concealed within any of the books which flanked the opposite wall, or within the back of the anglepoise lamp, or be monitoring her through one of the whorls of wallpaper that covered the left hand side of the room. The wallpaper was incongruous with the rest of the office. Yet the office itself seemed incongruous with the rest of Softwood.

She had been employed for over six months. It was a large, rambling estate, filled with intellectuals and scientists, set amongst several acres of woodland populated by both roe and muntjac deer. One of her roles was to decipher any meanings which might be found within the extracts of Linear A, yet she had made little progress. She was expert in Latin and Greek, had studied Linear B and considered Alice Kober to have been a role model, but the data that was available was simply insufficient to discern patterns. This was frustrating, but it was also interesting and the pay was good. Not only that, the company was even better. Being a residential establishment, the evenings at Softwood were filled with conversation which she found stimulating, never wondering why she was there.

The door opened and Grantham entered. She smiled and he acknowledged her with a nod before taking his seat opposite.

"Apricot."

"Mr Grantham."

She had seen him before, of course, but, as with the deer, not up close. She guessed that he was in his seventies; he had a good head of only slightly receding white hair, thick black-rimmed spectacles, a brown tie over a cream shirt, and his customary jacket which wasn't part of a suit. Unlike her, his clothes were mismatched. But this leant him a certain charm. In fact, Apricot was a little overawed. If this registered with Grantham it didn't show.

"I've been looking at your findings with Linear A," he began.

Apricot held back from voicing that *findings* might be a generous word.

"To be honest," he continued, "I'm rather disappointed."

She struggled to maintain her posture. So this was it, she was being discharged from her duties.

"I appreciate the source material is minimal, but we were rather hoping that someone with your previous experience might have been able to pull a rabbit out of the hat, as it were." He leant forwards, picked up a stray paperclip which he then unbent within his fingers and used to pick holes in the doodled green blotting paper which covered part of the desk. "Still, the disappointment isn't with you as such. You've proven to be a valuable member of the team. Roche speaks highly of you, as does Miss Cardamon. So highly, in fact, we've decided to offer you a new position, a unique position."

Apricot wondered if her relief showed. She would have been happy cleaning the ladies' rooms if it meant remaining in Softwood.

Grantham sat back in his chair, regarded the paperclip with curiosity, as if he hadn't seen it before. He placed it in his pocket. "The work we're considering is highly confidential. You will be isolated in a wing of Softwood and your movements will be limited. You won't come into contact with many – if any – of the acquaintances you have already made. Of course, if this isn't acceptable to you then we might have to let you go. Budgets are tight at the moment, and in six months..." he let his hands speak as they opened and their movement triggered his shoulders to shrug.

"I understand," said Apricot, her mind a whirl. "What is it you want me to do?"

A few days later she found herself hugging Miss Cardamon and giving Roche a playful wink.

"The secrets of Linear A will mean nothing without you," he said.

Thankfully she wasn't a girl for blushing. "If you decipher it," she said, "I hope to be the first to know."

Their smiles were warm. Roche came and put his arm around her shoulders, gave her a squeeze. "Of course," he said, then left the room quicker than she expected.

Miss Cardamon looked at her. "He has a crush on you."

"Maybe." Apricot detected the wistfulness in her voice.

Miss Cardamon looked as if she might say more, but then the door opened and Grantham's personal secretary nodded.

"If you're ready, follow me. Your luggage has already been taken care of."

She smiled as Miss Cardamon raised an eyebrow. "I'm being relocated both personally and professionally," Apricot said.

The last words she heard as she left the room were: "Don't be a stranger."

Apricot followed the secretary through the winding corridors of Softwood. Grantham's office had no windows as it was deep in the heart of the building, a nest within a nest of boxes. But on these floors the massive leaded windows of the former stately home shone copious amounts of light onto the highly polished floors and added to the grandeur of the building which was filled with artefacts and the unknown.

Apricot was no less swept away than she had been when she first arrived. A surge of adventure coursed through her, and she reminded herself how glad she was not to have travelled the beauty therapist, housewife, or even librarian route chosen by some of her contemporaries.

The secretary didn't speak. He avoided direct eye contact and kept himself to himself.

At the opposite end of the house, having passed fewer and fewer people along the way, the secretary unlocked a door which led to a stairwell.

"Your rooms are down there," he said. "Everything you need."

She nodded and waited for him to continue, but he simply held the door open. Eventually she realised he meant her to go down alone.

"Thank you," she said. Then she squeezed past him and her heels clicked out a rhythm on the stone stairway as she descended. It was a spiral. The constant turning proved disconcerting. It was just when she realised that she must be underground that she heard the door lock above her.

She paused and listened. There were no sounds. Knowing it would be churlish to return upstairs, she continued downwards. Without windows, electric light illuminated the way until eventually she reached the bottom.

If the stairway had seemed sterile, the corridor that

greeted her was welcoming. Thickly carpeted; with several rooms leading off to each side. At the end, an earthenware pot fired with a deep blue glaze stood on a small table beneath a mirror.

She walked towards it, expecting the corridor to branch either left or right at an angle which she couldn't yet see, but quickly realised the corridor was the extent of the space. She stood in front of the mirror, saw herself looking querulously back. Her curiosity was piqued. She returned down the corridor, trying each of the four doors as she went. They all opened. It seemed there were no secrets here.

She casually examined the rooms. The one nearest the foot of the stairway was her bedroom. The appearance was functional; she might have been at a budget hotel. Her bags had been laid on the bed and she spent time restoring normality by hanging her clothes in the wardrobe and placing her underwear and personal items in the bedside cabinet. The room across the corridor was the bathroom and toilet. The realisation hit home that she would be the only occupant in this part of the building, just as Grantham had promised. The thought both excited and scared her. Whatever she had been chosen for was indeed secret, yet she was a gregarious creature by nature.

The third room contained a computer and little else. The fourth room she was familiar with having done some radio assignments at college. All the right equipment was there for broadcasting.

On the middle of the desk in that room was a note.

She picked it up. It wasn't addressed to her. It bore the name *Vespertine.*

From now on, Vespertine *is your code name. Your only name.*

If we appear to be overly cautious please believe me there is a justifiable reason for this. The work you are to do is highly confidential. You have been chosen because of your background, your past experiences. Should you decide against this task, you can leave at any time. For the moment, however, please take a day or two to familiarise yourself with your surroundings. Your first broadcast won't be until midnight tomorrow evening.

Apricot read the note several times over. Over the course of two hours she had frequently walked up and down the stairwell, listening to nothing sounds on the other side of the locked door. Her reflection also revealed no answers. She felt like a lioness in a cage.

The letter was the only object in her quarters that she could interact with. The computer in the other room appeared to have no on/off switch and she realised its power was maintained elsewhere, independently. The letter confirmed this. From tomorrow and each day onwards she would be sent an email for that evening's broadcast. The letter made it clear there should be no deviation. It concluded: *Above all else we admire your professionalism.* It was signed, *William Grantham.*

Afterwards she found herself fiddling with the broadcasting equipment under the guise of familiarisation. There was no music saved on the hard drive which powered the mixing desk. The only file available was saved as *jingle.* When she opened it she heard the first two bars of the folk song, *The Lincolnshire Poacher,* played electronically. There was no soul in the song, but she knew why as soon as she heard it.

Apricot was to be the voice of a numbers station.

The door at the head of the stairs remained locked all night.

She had fully investigated all the rooms which led off the corridor by the time she went to sleep. In the room which housed the computer she realised there was a sliding panel that led to a dumb waiter. In it she found a tray holding a ploughman's lunch. While not feeling particularly hungry, she took the tray to her bed and ate heartily. Having opened the letter the dread she had initially felt began to dissipate. Even so, to be alone didn't sit well with her, and she found her thoughts continually turning to Roche.

Whilst she had no romantic liaisons during her six months at Softwood, Roche had played an increasing role in her fantasies. His broad shoulders, ready wit, natural intelligence and ease in her presence triggered everything that was female within her. Now, distant from him, she realised she should have eschewed her simmering shyness and played a wider role.

Come morning, she found the computer as awake as herself. A solitary email, under the name of *Grantham*, sat in her inbox. She opened it and saw a brief instruction together with the list of numbers she had been expecting. In every instance, the email stated, she should voice the final digit in each five number sequence with a lilt to her voice.

Apricot couldn't help but be intrigued. Numbers stations were known to her. She knew she would be broadcasting on various shortwave frequencies presumably controlled from outside of the environment she was in. Her voice would be artificially altered; synthesised. What she didn't know – what anyone didn't apparently know – was the purpose of these broadcasts. Although the speculation that she might be working for the British Secret Service sent a thrill up her spine that was hard to ignore.

She deliberated whether to respond to the email, then decided it wasn't necessary. She was sure all her movements must be under surveillance, although she hoped this didn't extend to the bedroom or bathroom.

Much of the day was spent looking into the mirror, practising her tone of voice for the broadcast, and repeatedly making the journey up and down the stairs to check that the door remained locked.

At eleven-thirty pm she initiated checks of the equipment, donned her headphones, and ensured the loudness of her voice was within the boundaries specified in the email.

At midnight she played the jingle.

At fifteen seconds past midnight, she began her broadcast.

0-2-5-8-8
6-9-7-2-1
3-0-1-1-2
9-0-2-3-6
4-4-5-7-3
2-0-0-0-7

The broadcast concluded at one am.

Apricot signed off as directed, a few seconds after the final number, with the solitary word: *vespertine.*

She smiled and switched off the equipment. Assuming they believed she had done her job satisfactorily, she imagined she would repeat the same task tomorrow.

In case you are wondering, the word vespertine *relates to a genus of flowers which only bloom in the evening.*

Apricot re-read the note which had been placed on her breakfast tray. It had been typed on an old fashioned typewriter. She could feel the indentations on the reverse of the paper, and the '*e*'s were blocked with excess ink.

She wondered who had sent this. Imagined it couldn't be Grantham, yet found it hard to believe his secretary was responsible. Nonsensically, she found herself hoping it had been Roche. And the sensation that he could have chosen her codename appealed to her.

After breakfast she drifted into a dreamless sleep. The day yawned before her. She began to think how long the task might last. Considered it could be indefinite. Searching the rooms she realised she had no way to communicate with the rest of Softwood. There were no writing implements, the computer would print the contents of the email but wouldn't open programs for anything else, and it had been clear on her first arrival that there was no signal for her mobile.

Again, a sense of panic coupled with excitement

gripped her. Whilst she was – in some respects – solely in control of her destiny, she realised this was completely within imposed parameters. *So this is what religion feels like*, she thought. The sense of predetermination was as comforting as it was compelling.

Days began to slide into one. A succession of numbers. No other notes accompanied her breakfast or any other meal, and the emails from constantly changing accounts contained less and less comment and more and more numbers. Her broadcasts became equally uniform:

5-5-3-2-7
6-8-4-3-2
3-3-2-2-3
0-9-0-2-1
1-2-1-1-2
0-0-0-0-0

The one certainty – she had to remind herself – was that the task held purpose and that her contribution was valued.

She had to remind herself over and again.

Apricot became a creature of habit. She set herself routines to deal with the day and allowed transformation to occur during the evening. She reasoned that if she were Apricot whilst the sun was up, so she should be Vespertine as it set. She began to dress accordingly, choosing items from her wardrobe which could delineate between the two personalities. Apricot: the diligent, demure employee. Vespertine: the spy and potential femme fatale. In perpetuating this format, she effectively halved her days.

Mornings she cleansed her face with a salt facial scrub in the bathroom mirror, washed her skin clean until it was as smooth as stone. She wore the professional skirt suit in which she had attended Grantham's interview, and imagined the one-way exchange she had with the computer as if she were dealing with clients in a tax office. Come evening, she glammed up from the contents of her make-up bag, overly rouging her lips, choosing clothes she reserved for the occasional decadent party, using the corridor as a catwalk as she sauntered back and forth towards the earthenware pot and the mirror above it. Wondered if Roche could witness her transformation, or whether it was only Grantham who wondered what he had done.

9-2-4-3-2
4-4-6-7-2
0-9-7-2-7
2-8-2-7-4
7-4-8-6-3

Apricot began to find her relationship with Vespertine was a destructive one. Compared to her mundane lifestyle waiting around for something to happen, Vespertine's was one of glamour and public presence. Vespertine was the one who existed beyond the corridor and its four rooms. Vespertine had a life which extended to all corners of the globe, her voice reaching anyone who tuned in, and possibly affecting some of those listeners deeply, personally; whereas Apricot's circle of influence was limited, her interactions all one way: either electronically through email or via the dumb waiter returning empty plates.

One morning, after a shower, after wondering how many showers she had taken downstairs during how many mornings, Apricot remembered that Roche wasn't simply an object of fantasy for Vespertine's occasionally tremulous outbursts, but that he had been a linguist working with her to solve the Linear A code.

The *language* was written on fragments of stone tablets, a Cretan writing system found at Knossos alongside a later language eventually decoded and known as Linear B.

It was then that Apricot gathered together the printed lists of numbers she had retained in what she had designated to be an out-tray beside the broadcasting equipment and gave herself the task of deciphering the meaning.

Within the confines of the rooms which now constituted her existence, she began to unravel the meaning of her life.

A smile returned to Apricot's face which was borrowed from Vespertine's.

She poured herself into the numbers. Made lists of those which occurred more frequently than others. Equated the frequent numbers with some of the more popular vowels. Broke each set of numbers into smaller sets and merged some of the sequences together. She had to do this literally, tearing up the paper and reforming it in a collage. Before she left Softwood she was determined to know its secrets. Her days began to recapture the intrigue she had first found at being there. Apricot began to consider herself a match for Vespertine.

After a number of indeterminate days fraught with frustration, she returned her breakfast toast to the dumb waiter with the crusts shaped to spell *pen*.

The implement arrived with her evening meal.

5-5-6-4-3

7-8-3-6-3

1-1-2-3-2

1-8-7-6-3

0-3-5-0-0

Vespertine signed off, removed her headphones, and gazed into her image dulled by the blackness of the monitor. She listened intently. As usual, apart from a low hum associated with the equipment, her rooms were silent. She focussed on the image of a spy she had created, the one who was eagerly listening to and transcribing her broadcasts. He was broad shouldered, carried humour with his intelligence, not unlike Roche. She wondered what Roche would think of her now, if she ascended the stairs and found the door open. Surely he couldn't equate her with the mousy Apricot? Surely there would be no holding back.

She rose from the desk and went to stand in the

corridor before the mirror. She wore an ankle length black dress, low cut at the front and also at the back. Her lips were rouged and mascara visibly dripped from her eyelashes. She wanted to dye her brunette hair black, to complete the ensemble. Instead she leant forwards and imprinted a kiss on the mirror, left it for Apricot to clean, before she made her way languorously to bed, wishing Roche were watching her every step.

Start with the number you first thought of.

Apricot woke to find her head laying on a sheaf of papers. The printed numbers were underscored in blue ink. Arrows pointed from one to another, like a map of international airways. She rubbed sleep out of the corners of her eyes and stumbled across to the bathroom to splash water on her face, stepping over a black dress she couldn't remember discarding.

Emerging from the bathroom in vest top and pants she returned to the numbers. They swam independently of her gaze. She squeezed her eyes tight, opened them again. The numbers refused to remain static. She shook her head, but the jumbling remained. *I'm going crazy*, she thought. *There's something I'm not seeing.*

The realisation made her sit bolt upright.

Might it not be the numbers which were the key to the code, but the spaces between?

She ran down the corridor to the radio room. Vespertine had recorded each and every broadcast. Apricot donned her headphones and played them back, as many as she could to confirm her suspicions. She could hear tones in the background which hadn't been evident when the broadcasts were made. Could it be that the voice was simply an aid to tuning into the correct frequency, with the actual coded message being sent by modulating the tones, such as with burst transmission?

She shook her head. There was more to it than that.

She focused on the spaces between the sets of numbers, on the hiss of white noise, the gradation in tones. She suddenly tore off the headset. She had heard *voices*, she had heard words being transmitted between the numbers.

Still in her vest and pants she ran up the spiral staircase and banged her fists on the door until the skin came off her knuckles.

She slid to the ground, leant tight into the corner. Vespertine found her that way when evening came.

She picked her up. Carried her down the staircase. Into the domain of ghosts.

3-4-5-6-7

3-2-5-6-7

7-8-6-2-2

When Apricot woke she found herself on the floor of the broadcasting suite. Adjacent to her, Vespertine was reading numbers off a sheet of paper, her voice inflecting at the end of each series of five.

2-3-2-3-1

7-6-5-4-3

2-4-5-7-8

Apricot moved into a sitting position, her back against the wall. She rubbed her eyes, bit the inside of her mouth. Vespertine kept reading numbers, until eventually she signed off with that single word.

She turned to face her. "We're working on different things," she said, her voice echoed, as if in a dream. "Your job is to understand the numbers, mine is to detect ghosts through electronic voice perception. Whilst I read the numbers, the machine records. The machine records everything. The voice tunes the channel. Don't you see how that works?"

"I need out," said Apricot, softly.

"We both need out, darling."

Vespertine's voice was low and throaty. Apricot goosebumped.

"You're not on the floor," Vespertine said.

Apricot's hair was tied tight at the back of her head. She sat in the chair in Grantham's office. Roche stood behind her, with one hand on her shoulder as if he were holding her down. In reality, she appreciated the comfort.

"Because of you," Grantham was saying, "a lot of lives have been saved. I'm sorry we had to keep details from you. Roche and I considered that if you had simply been given the task of decoding the numbers from the outset, then the chances of success would be lessened. Your talents are not inconsiderable, but Roche was right when he insinuated a frisson of absolute determination should be injected into the work. I hope – in retrospect – that makes sense."

Apricot nodded. It had been two days since she was released from the cellar, over five weeks since her conversation with Vespertine. She considered charges of unlawful detention, but with the brains of the country against her and issues of national security at risk, she knew nothing would come of it.

She had never been broadcasting the numbers. She had been given numbers already broadcast, and then coerced into a situation where she felt compelled to decode them. But this didn't explain the voices. Grantham and Roche knew nothing about them. She kept them as quiet as Vespertine.

"A vacation is needed," smiled Grantham; the look sat odd on his face. "Your choice."

Away, thought Apricot. *Away*, thought Vespertine. They needed to be away from Softwood and all the covert activities it contained, some of which only they knew.

But *away* wasn't where the discoveries would be made, where the satisfaction would come. They had tapped into knowledge that couldn't be hidden, which they needed to nurture to reap its full potential. That was where the acclaim lay: not with Linear A, nor decoding the numbers. But in the terrible secrets of Softwood revealed by the ghosts. Those harboured by Grantham and Roche.

"I'll stay," Apricot said. She saw Vespertine nod. They would remain to destroy that which they loved.

Soleil

Adele Kirby

I

She went by the name of Soleil. Previous aliases included the masculine as well as the feminine, not to mention various honorific titles and impersonal alpha-numeric codes. She was 'Wanted' – with definite capitalisation – although quietly, on secret databases seen only by the Sauris System's version of the 00 agent: serious people with polite words such as 'enforcer', 'counter-intelligence' and 'exempt from the rules of law' in their job descriptions. She had been one of those also, in her time.

She was terrifyingly competent in all matters of violence. She was difficult to find and harder still to bait. And on this particular occasion, she was wearing a dress that made her impossible to miss. It did not so much hug as caress the female form, of which hers was a fine example; the kind of creation that made every woman subconsciously tug down or hoist up her own dress as appropriate, and made every man want to dig his fingers through its sleek, shining folds to experience the terrain of the taut body below.

In short, the dress was as subtle as a punch to the stomach. And it had a similar physiological impact on the world at large: whether of lust or envy, it caused many a shortening of breath as Soleil proceeded, with the sort of sensual grace liable to cause traffic accidents, between the space dock and the Excelsius Pavilion. Someone had thrown a gala party in the most prestigious venue in the Galactic

State for the sole purpose of gaining her attention. It seemed only fair to dress to impress, so she had done so in a colour that was the bold match of her nails, the exact shade of her lips, the vivid scarlet of blood spilled on snow.

II

He answered to the name Eclipse. Even he could not recall all the names he had assumed in a lifetime that exceeded the cycle of stars. He had watched civilisations rise and fall, like so many waves erasing footprints in sand. Few folk knew enough about him to know how Wanted he would be if they did. Names he had worn and deeds he had done echoed through stories shared between the planets of the Sauris System – but individually, unconnected, as anonymous as the face he wore now.

He knew everything there was to know about staying alive in the physical sense; it was staving off the mental boredom of ages that presented the challenge. . There was little that he wanted and only one thing that he needed. On the occasion of their historic encounter, he was working as a waiter at the most famous venue in the Sauris Galactic State. At a party, arranged at his behest solely for the benefit of a woman who was not even technically invited. The event had been unwittingly funded by several powerful figures with shadowy connections to Sauris' largest organised crime syndicates, all of whom were present and drinking away in blissful ignorance of their own generosity.

He was a very good waiter, and worked the room like an artiste. Flowing amongst his guests, he casually spread misinformation about their mysterious host, flirted good-naturedly with women, irrespective of their beauty, mentally archived juicy gossip for future use, and eavesdropped on many a conversation not meant for his ears. Within half an hour he was perfectly attuned to the pulse of the crystalline space pavilion, such that he was aware of the cardiac spikes caused by the new arrival long before he laid eyes on her himself.

Eclipse first stood very still, absently wiping pristine crystal glasses with a soft cloth, feeling the subtle – and, in some cases, less subtle – shifts in the soul of the party as it reacted to the presence of Soleil. He nodded approvingly to himself, for before even seeing her, he knew the colour of her dress: *scarlet red*. Like lying lips, the blood of the dying, or the flaming heart of a sun.

III

Eclipse subtly shifted his serving patterns to follow the ripples left by his prey: an old and practiced strategy which ought to have brought him into her vicinity in minutes. Instead, she proved inspiringly elusive. It would not, of course, be within the rules of the engagement to ask his guests whether they had seen the woman in the killer red dress. He had expected her to loiter with elegant intent, allowing her innate magnetism to draw him to her -- but instead, she seemed to be working the room herself, and better even than he did. He was quietly pleased to have to work for this. Everywhere he went, she had already been, leaving a trail of bothered women forced to work at competing for the attention of their distracted men. Masking sheer joy under a professionally polished veneer, Eclipse paused at a buffet table to reload his tray with eye-wateringly expensive champagne, distilled from the vapours of a supernova, while mentally mapping the crowded space.

He sensed her presence behind him just a fraction before he noticed the distracted ripple spreading out ahead. Oh, she was *good*. She had made herself both easy and impossible to track. That she had found him in the meantime was so much more impressive than he could have hoped.

Savouring the moment, he continued precisely as he

was, meticulously placing the last six glasses onto his tray. She had caught him out, but he would make her wait for her prize.

"Champagne, my lady?" he asked, turning and proffering the tray in one movement. And there she was: exactly as magnificent as he had imagined. Tall, proud, patient. A woman with all the time in the world.

"Too kind."

Her voice was rich and smooth, like the brush of newly spun silk against bare skin, and without the throaty purr which often cut the tone of powerful women. She took the nearest glass, but did not drink, which made it harder for Eclipse to examine her within the bounds of polite behaviour. He was, after all, still a servant, until proven otherwise. But look he did, and what he saw were flinty silver eyes set into a sculpted face that was, disconcertingly, both familiar and strange. Soleil had deftly twisted her hair into an impressive arrangement from which rogue strands escaped, falling in fine amber ringlets over pale skin.

"Perhaps you would prefer another drink?" he asked, indicating a wider selection of choices from the buffet table. "An Orion Starburst? Some distilled amphimel nectar?." Or perhaps this rather unusual beverage?" He poured from an elegant silver tube. Two liquids emerged, one a rich dark brown, the other white. The two mixed in the glass, swirling together to release both steam and the most tantalising aroma. "I believe it's called 'coffee'," he said.

Soleil curiously exchanged her champagne for the proffered glass, a delicate crystal flute, now warm to the touch. She sipped, cautiously – and though her face immediately contorted, she admirably managed to swallow.

"Where did you find *that?*" she gasped, examining the aftertaste with a kind of fascinated horror.

"A small planet across the galaxy, accessible via wormhole only every decade or so," Eclipse replied, charmingly servile. "Your host has spared no expense."

"He could have spared us all this," she said, exchanging the flute for the champagne glass once more. "Tell me, is our mysterious host as reclusive as they say?" She fixed Eclipse with the most direct look woman has ever bestowed upon man. He felt exposed in its path, but had no idea just how sub the text might be. If she was indeed his target, probably not very. If she wasn't, her efforts would, alas, be wasted on him.

"I believe 'private' is a more accurate term," he said diplomatically.

She sipped the delicate liquid, but her eyes never left him. "Only a determinedly lonely man would choose to inflict the joy of others upon his solitude so."

"You see this as an occasion of joy?" Eclipse asked, genuinely curious. Soleil finally released him from her piercing attention, turning her gaze instead on the party at large. Eclipse followed suit, taking in the faces surrounding them. What he saw was the Sauris upper crust at its most pretentious, the women decked in gaudy dresses and glittering jewels, the men working the current dark and mysterious look as though colour were a crime against cool. Soleil wore colour fearlessly, like a beacon in the darkness, and Eclipse – he wore black as though he were a living shadow, which was not so far from the truth.

IV

Looking upon the exact same room, but through her golden eyes, Soleil saw a different scene altogether. She was entertained by the manner in which her dress disarmed men, felt sympathy for the women she disconcerted, wished relief for those whose party was not going as planned, and was pleased by the laughter that rang around her. She smiled upon most of what she saw – a strange little expression, broken at the edges by sadness and envy.

"I do see joy," she said finally, turning back to the

waiter. "Just because I cannot share in such lightness of spirit myself, does not mean I resent it in others."

He took that well enough instead of falling back on the defensiveness typical of most men, and this strengthened her suspicions. She was not yet, after all, certain he was her target. Images of Eclipse did not exist, but her research had been comprehensive.

She turned from the activity of the pavilion to observe the bright aura of Ozai, rotating lazily below the massive viewing windows for which the Pavilion was so famous. Ancient Ozai: once home to the Aurealus, birthplace of the Age of Angels, a planet destroyed by its own internal war a thousand years ago, and ravaged still by fires which would burn a thousand years more until every flammable gas in the land and atmosphere had been finally consumed. From space, the Planet of Fire was a sight of such breath-taking beauty that it was easy to forget its horrific past.

V

It was not a coincidence that Eclipse had so carefully arranged to meet Soleil here, and in her face, lit by the stratospheric glow of the burning planet, he could see that she too knew this to be true. Also, that she was waiting for his next move.

"Would you look at that: your TBS scanner isn't working," she said casually, without even turning. Her words came exactly as Eclipse discovered the malfunction for himself. "Shame, that." She smiled winningly. "Now you have no idea what I am."

This was intriguing for three reasons: firstly that he had designed the trans-bio signature scanner himself, and knew the exact locations of each of the very rare – and even more expensive – three models in existence. Secondly, the scan was retinally activated, so he was certain he had not given away its use.

"And here it's been operating perfectly all night until now," he said, equally casually, even though until that moment, he would have bet body parts that the technology to disrupt the TBS did not yet exist in Sauris.

Thirdly, she had indeed routed his most accurate method for identifying who – and, as she had rightly pointed out, what – she was.

"Clever technology for a table waiter," she observed.

"Sophisticated defence for an invited guest," he replied, placing his tray safely on the buffet table.

She smiled. "I do hope that wasn't the only clever trick up your sleeve."

"Of course not. I'll show you mine, if you show me yours." Eclipse patted an inconspicuous bulge in his neat jacket.

Soleil was less concerned than disillusioned. "A gun? Really?"

"Your hands where I can see them, please."

"You're making two poor assumptions here," she said. "The first, that I have in fact been invited." She raised her hands. "The second, that you're the only person here with retinal relay contact lenses ."

Eclipse promptly shot Soleil, and was intensely disappointed when she went down.

VI

The first thing Soleil saw when she opened her eyes was a picture of melancholy. Eclipse sat just feet away, sloped forward, chin on his hands, watching her. Her hands were tied behind a gilded chair, its ornamentation biting into her arms. Her legs, however, were elegantly crossed. She suspected she ought to feel a slight thrill about this, but was unable to do so. She knew she ought to feel nauseous as a result of the stun ray, so blinked with faux grogginess and put on an appropriately unimpressed face. She did however spare them both the understandable but dull 'What is the meaning of this?' dialogue.

"This hasn't gone to plan, has it?" she asked instead.

"Not entirely, no," Eclipse agreed.

"You were expecting someone else?" she asked, after they had sized one another up a little too long.

"Some*thing* else, yes," Eclipse said. "The stun would only have worked against organic life forms. It would not have worked against my target."

"You thought I was, what... an AI?" Soleil provocatively extended a sculpted leg. "I don't know whether to be flattered or offended."

"She is a remarkable piece of work. A unique achievement that rivals even you in both looks and skill," he assured her.

"Then I shall choose to be flattered. You have gone to a great deal of effort to find her: I am sorry to disappoint." Soleil cocked her head to one side, contemplating her situation. "What is it you want with her? You strike me as an intellectual villain: I appear to be quite unravaged."

"You assume that I am the villain of the piece." Eclipse looked, if anything, weary at the suggestion.

"Well, as the only person in the room who has been shot and tied to a chair, I'm struggling to see you in a heroic light," Soleil replied coolly. "Lack of ravaging aside, that is. For which I thank you."

"You're welcome."

"Though if you'd like to try –?"

"I'm sure I can restrain myself,"

"You don't find me attractive?" Soleil shot back.

"That's not what I said." He paused. "But... you find me attractive?"

"I find you intriguing, which is much more interesting. But given a choice between being shot and tied up some more and ravaged, I'll take the latter, if it's all the same to you."

"Ravaging is not really my style."

"Being tied up isn't really mine though, either." Soleil lifted her no-longer-bound hands "You don't mind?"

Eclipse frowned, but said, "Be my guest."

"Thank you." She rubbed circulation back into her reddened wrists. "So, your target. She is the villain of this story?"

He paused before answering, as if choosing his words carefully. "She is a danger, yes."

"To whom?"

"To you."

Soleil lifted an already arched eyebrow.

"To me, to everyone," he continued. "To the future of this galaxy."

"And is she this dangerous by intent? Or involuntarily, by design?" Soleil asked. "She is an Artificial Intelligence, after all. She is as she is made."

"She is something more. Something special." Eclipse stood quickly. "And she is my concern, not yours. I apologise for wasting your time. I will not impose on you further. Please, avail yourself of my more civil hospitality back in the pavilion."

Soleil ignored his politely directing arm.

"What will you do to her, if you find her?"

"When," he corrected, still waiting for her to leave. "When I find her, I will do what must be done. Without malice, prejudice or pleasure."

Soleil rose. She pulled her dress down to a point of passable modesty, and proceeded with long, languid steps towards Eclipse, her heels *click, click, clicking* across the polished floor. With supple hips swaying and immaculately defined legs almost crossing stride by stride, hers was the stalk of the feline huntress. It would take a strong man to remain e/motionless in the face of that approach. Eclipse, however, did not so much as flinch, even when her red lips were inches from his ear, her breath warm upon his cheek.

"Then I think we have reached an understanding," she whispered.

VII

Eclipse moved with impressive speed. At such, he should have been easily able to twist, snake one arm around Soleil's neck, lock her wrists with the other and drop her to her knees within seconds. Soleil, however, reacted even more quickly. Eclipse's lock closed on thin air: she had already anticipated his move. Rather than simply evading, she turned his own action against him, and it was Eclipse who ended up on his knees.

He briefly tested her iron grip, and she didn't doubt that against a normal woman, even most men, he could have extracted himself with comparative ease. But Soleil was not normal. Arguably, she was not technically a woman either.

She could have broken his neck then, and they both knew it. But she did not.

"Finish it!" he said grimly. "Otherwise you have my word that I will keep hunting you."

"And I will keep evading you." She let him go. He was on his feet immediately, coming at her with speed, skill and agility. And she did, indeed, simply keep evading him. But Eclipse was a worthy adversary and she pitied him his mortal disadvantage, so she chose to route the stalemate. She froze, when she ought to have moved. He smashed a hand against her shoulder. The sound almost as sickening as the shock of pain.

"I do not wish to, Eclipse... but eventually, if I have to, I will kill you," she said, without malice, prejudice or pleasure. "I have hundreds of years' experience in this matter."

"Against my thousands of years of staying alive? You will need them, Soleil," he said, though nursing his broken hand.

Thousands of years? Soleil's research had suggested that the body Eclipse wore was not his own, but this was unexpected, if not impossible.

"Tell me who you are," she said.

"You know I cannot."

Soleil nodded. Anywhere in Sauris, the truth of her identity would cost her freedom if not her life. She understood entirely.

"I think I know someone who can, though," she said, almost apologetically. "Everyone has a leverage point."

Eclipse looked entertained at this idea. "I think you'll find I have long since run out of levers."

"There's always one. I'm sorry."

Soleil blinked, activating a retinal relay response: a sharp electrical pulse from her ship that momentarily interrupted the brain activity of every living creature on the Pavilion. Throughout the gala party, guests experienced momentary dizzy turns and nausea. Eclipse, however, collapsed.

VIII

Like a puppet with cut strings, his legs simply gave way. The moment he hit the ground, Soleil hauled him back up to his knees, her face now hard: there was no time to play.

"Wakey wakey," she ordered. The body that Eclipse formerly wore stirred slowly, but it was another person looking back at her now through normal, confused, grey-blue eyes.

"Wha... What happened...?" not-Eclipse managed, clearly disoriented and distressed.

"I just happened to Eclipse. You're home alone right now. You can thank me later."

With one arm, Soleil lifted him bodily by the collar and dumped him unceremoniously back on his chair.

"Focus. Now," she ordered. The man's gaze started the

climb from her waist to her face, but became side-tracked along the way by the inviting depth of her cleavage.

"On *me*," she growled, adding a sharp slap for effect. He groaned. She sighed, and straddled him. He stiffened bodily between her legs, this time with a small gasp, but he was alert at least.

"This is strictly between you and me, you understand?" she said. "He won't understand."

The man nodded.

"Who is Eclipse?"

To his credit, the helpless man managed a defiant shake of the head. Soleil shifted her hips slightly and reached to grip him intimately before repeating the question. Not-Eclipse blanched.

"He is… a caretaker."

"Of what?"

"Of everything," he moaned. "Would you mind just letting go of…?"

"I'm not done yet," she snapped, giving a quick, sharp squeeze. "What does that mean? Caretaker of everything?"

"He keeps the future – free of the past."

"Why? What past?"

In answer, the wretched man managed to twist enough to look at the burning planet below. Soleil followed his gaze, and suddenly, she understood. Who Eclipse was. Why he had brought her here, of all places.

"He is... Aurealus...?"

Not-Eclipse nodded, his face pleading. She released her grip – only for him to convulse, his pale eyes rolling horribly into the top of his eye sockets. When they returned, the irises were the gold of Eclipse. The same colour as Soleil's own, concealed under her silver retinal relay contact lenses.

The state of the body gripped between her thighs changed entirely, from wild stimulation to the tension of a coiled spring.

Eclipse was angry.

Soleil no longer knew what she was, literally or emotionally. She remained frozen upon his lap. She knew he would be reading everything he needed to know, but she didn't have it in her to hide a thing.

IX

As he read the conflict in her face, Eclipse softened. Soleil, in her turn, sagged, the crown of her head falling to rest again his chest, strands of her hair running down his shirt. The body he wore suffered an automated response, but he himself felt nothing. He wondered whether he ought to pat her back.

He did not.

"I take it you have the answer to your question," he said, finally.

Soleil released her legs and pushed back off him: the straddled position was hideously inappropriate now.

"You played well," Eclipse said respectfully. "Faking unconsciousness to the stun was inspired."

"You weren't fooled though," she replied hollowly.

"No. But I had to bait you further to be sure."

"And I needed to know what you wanted of me."

"And now that you do?"

Soleil walked slowly to the viewing window, so that Osai filled her world.

"Tell me a story?" she asked, and bravely, because it could not be a story she wanted to hear. She sensed Eclipse's presence close behind her. It was strangely calming. He would destroy her, but she intuitively knew he would do so with fair warning. And without malice, prejudice or pleasure.

"There was once a beautiful planet called Osai," he started. "Its people fought and loved and strove and failed and fought again, and after thousands of years of conflict, they found peace."

"The Age of Angels," Soleil said, quietly.

"Indeed. They built magnificent cities, terraformed other worlds into the likeness of Osai and engineered extraordinary things. The pinnacle of their achievement: the Aurealus, Artificial Emotional Intelligence so advanced, so sophisticated, it could be mistaken for its own creators."

"And the world knew war again," Soleil finished. Every child of the Sauris System knew the basic fable – though Soleil of course had no childhood she could call her own.

She turned to Eclipse.

"And I make you think of that?" she asked.

"You are beautiful, Soleil. But when I see you, I see my planet burn."

"I will never let that happen."

He smiled sadly, and gently brushed her cheek.

"It is beautiful naivety that you think you have a choice in the matter."

"I am not Aurealus!" she insisted. "And I am no army. I am alone."

"You are not. Sauris has developed the technology to recreate AEI such as you a dozen times over. For thousands of years I have sabotaged such plans – but Soleil, I missed you." He shrugged, apologetic and resolute all at once. "You cannot exist. You must not exist. Osai is my reminder of the fact."

"Is that is why you brought me here? To show me my ancestry?"

"To show you your destiny. The potential for which you were created."

He was not being cruel, and she could not hate him for a truth.

"The first of the Aurealus meant no harm either. I would undo its existence also, had I but the power to. I ask nothing of you that I would not do myself."

Soleil looked heavily upon him then, the first of the Aurealus – at least what remained – and he saw himself as she must: a program so sophisticated it had become the literal ghost in the machine, a spirit that could transcend the physical shell. A tired soul that looked back at her through the eyes of a mortal man hijacked to a life of service to an age old duty.

"I wear the blood of many dead and dying on my hands," she said slowly. "It was for murder that I was created. It was for death that I lived; but now, I have a soul, and it is of the living that I dream."

"Your existence jeopardises theirs. I am sorry, Soleil. You are but an angle in a ruthless geometry of destruction."

Soleil returned to her seat. She sat back down, crossed her fine legs, raised her hands, and told Eclipse to do what he must.

X

Eclipse too sat down again, watching her gravely.

"I give you my permission," she insisted, in the face of his hesitation. "I can even tell you how – although I am sure you already know."

"I too wear the blood of many on my hands," he said, as though trying to explain himself.

"I know. I have heard it said that through great suffering comes great strength." Soleil had learned this through one of her earlier incarnations. The memory of the lesson hurt her still. There was no power to be gained from inflicting suffering on others, but being the cause of it armoured the soul – even an artificial one – crushing it within hardened plates of guilt. And in Soleil – as in Eclipse – responsibility had forged a desperate, aching need for atonement. Right now, facing death, she felt that strength, born of suffering. Felt the strongest she ever had.

For his part, and not for the first time, Eclipse found himself grappling with the bitterest of irony: that his redemption for causing the suffering of countless millions lay in the taking of yet another life. Soleil was indeed the closest he had to kin. She had rightly identified the host of the gala as lonely, but then, she would know all too well the bite of agelessness, of never being able to go home. Of having no home to go to. It occurred to him, looking upon her beautiful, flawless face, that they might be the two loneliest creatures in the universe.

He realised he could not take her life, for her sake or his own.

"There is one other solution," he suddenly realised out loud. "Soleil – come with me. Travel with me."

Soleil stared at him.

"And do what, exactly?" she demanded.

"Oh, you know. Trounce evil. Put the worlds to right." His eyes brightened at the idea.

"So you can supervise me? That's going to save the world?"

"Where I'm going, I won't need to," he said, on his feet once more. "All I need is to take you out of Sauris. So let's go and explore this interesting little planet no one is supposed to know about, on the other side of the galaxy, accessible by an untethered wormhole for a couple of seconds every decade or so, and next in..." he checked his watch "...about three days' time."

Eclipse smiled from his soul: the first time he had done so in at least the last century. He extended one hand. Slowly, Soleil took it, and allowed him to draw her to the viewing window.

"It doesn't have to happen again. We'll go where no one has heard of the Aurealus, where they drink coffee and you and I will have no more history than destiny."

"A new world?" Soleil considered. It was a temptation. "Is it dangerous?"

"Mostly harmless, as I understand."

"I bore easily," Soleil warned.

"I'm sure we're both due a holiday. Somewhere we have

no-one to hide from." Eclipse glanced through the viewing screen. "Somewhere free of the shadow of Osai."

"How unreliable is the wormhole?"

"Oh, very. It could be an extremely long holiday."

Soleil felt lighter already.

"Can I trust you, Eclipse?"

"Not for a moment," he said cheerfully. She nodded. Just the way she liked it.

Earth would, in time, cost Soleil yet another name and both of them their current faces. And these would be considered a price worth paying. For when first they met, they were two souls lonelier than a dying star; cursed by their sentience, they remembered better times now lost, and would remember them still for aeons yet to come. But in each other, there in the glow of old Osai, they found a kinship for the cursed.

New adventures beckoned. Dreams of freedom stirred. Together they stood in silence, bidding what they thought were farewells to the planet of the dead, their artificial eyes reflecting the play of leaping flares, cavorting across the surface of a planet as beautiful and deadly as the burning heart of a sun.

Haecceity

Stewart Hotston

He was waved through by an armed policeman at the perimeter. Faizul was standing on the other side of the shivering yellow cordon of inch wide tape. "Morning boss. You're not going to believe this."

"C'mon then," said Michael. He stepped gingerly through the unending detritus of pulverised wood, glass and waste paper that always covered the site of every explosion he'd ever worked. The end of human civilisation was non-descript rubbish. The wreckage was beyond recovery and too vast a volume to begin imagining the clean up that would inevitably occur once they were done with forensics. Amazingly, the building was still standing, reinforced concrete struts peeking through the damp mist and floating debris as he negotiated his way around shattered masonry.

By the time they reached the point of interest, Michael was trudging through the mess without a second thought. In spite of himself he was amazed; a girl lay, without burns, in the recovery position while paramedics attended.

"First responder Darren Hall found her under a ton of roof. Got the fright of his life when she shouted out as he poked around between collapsed joists." Faizul was reading from notes, peering occasionally over the top of his pocket book to look at the girl. "Lapsing in and out of consciousness, hasn't said a word. Duty physician is Josh Cohn." Michael nodded. He knew the man, mid-forties, career in public service.

"Have you met him before?" he asked Faizul.

His sergeant shook his head. "No, Sir."

"Word of advice, he's seen more blood than Dracula. It's left him with a unique view of the world."

"I've met my share of pathologists and morticians," said Faizul dismissively.

Michael shrugged. He didn't care to babysit and had warned his man about the desert-dry doctor. The rest was down to him. Waving over one of the white scene suited SOCOs he said, "Where's Dr. Cohn?"

The eyes of the woman behind the mask rolled and with a turn of the head she indicated deeper into the site, through a partially pulverised doorway. Faizul followed after him, taking photos on his phone. They found Cohn talking to another medic. The Attending was tall and thin with a greying moustache hanging heavily and untrimmed over his top lip. Like SOCO he was wearing a white suit, although his face was uncovered.

"More survivors?" asked Michael, interrupting Cohn in mid-flow. The doctor ignored him and finished his conversation. Michael didn't say anything else.

Cohn turned to Michael, "Ya wee shite, did your mother teach you nae manners?" His voice was like three day old cigarette smoke.

"I'm a disappointment to my mother in so many ways," said Michael.

"Aye," said Cohn approvingly. "Seen the wee bairn with nae a scratch on her?" Michael nodded. "What ye won't have seen was the man she must hae been with."

"Where's he?" asked Faizul, looking over his shoulder to where they had come from.

"Well, big man, I'd say he's on ye shoes, ye troos and pretty much spread across the rest of the site. If yer lucky, yon white suited minions might find his teeth. Now shut yer hole while the big boys talk, eh?"

"So what protected her from ending up like him?" asked Michael.

"Honestly, Michael?" suddenly his accent faded, "I've

no idea. I've never seen anything like it. The forensic pathologist will give you their best shot but I'd bet my daughter's Pooh Bear onesie that they'll not draw a firm conclusion. She was next to the site of the explosion. There is no reasonable explanation at this point for why she's still in one piece, let alone breathing."

"You're not Scottish!" said Faizul, the words bursting out from his mouth.

Cohn looked at him like a snake might regard a mouse. "Aye? Is that so? You being second generation Asian an' all would be the fucking expert on matters such as these, eh? Inspector, take your toddler off with ye, I've got work ta do."

Michael tried not to laugh as he led his fuming sergeant away.

"How long has she been waiting?" he asked the desk sergeant.

The overweight and faintly fusty man on duty looked at the computer screen, although Michael knew he must have been here when she arrived. "She was brought in about eleven this morning."

"Which room?"

"Two."

"Thanks. Can we get some coffees?"

"Sure," said the officer. Michael nodded and turned to find the interview room. "Machine's by reception," the sergeant said to his back. "Takes shrapnel and doesn't give change."

"I'll get them, gov," said his constable, Eleanor Stryck, before walking off to find them drinks.

"Get a tea for the interviewee," called Michael after her.

The interview room was standard issue mottled grey. There was a cctv in one corner, a single laminated chip board table with four chrome legged chairs. A stopped-up plug sat alone in the wall; it would once have had a tape recorder attached to it. The light was a thin fluorescent bar; the cool illumination creating gloom all around.

He was immediately struck by a smell he couldn't identify. Hints of apple, lavender and freesia, cinnamon and other spices he knew but couldn't name. It was so pleasant he took a second breath to try and retain its essence for as long as possible. Michael stopped himself from standing there and simply breathing only by dint of focussing on the witness they were supposed to be interviewing.

"Not what you expect in a cell, is it," said the woman.

Michael shook his head, almost groggy; it was as if he were fighting with himself to simply find a chair and sit.

"I'm sorry," he said after he had taken his seat, "I'm Inspector Michael Case. We'll be joined momentarily by my colleague, Constable Stryck." She didn't say anything. Her name was Jayne Seeker, 31, currently working as an accountant for one of the big four. Speciality was, according to the firm's website, IPV and illiquid asset valuation. He wasn't sure what that meant, even after looking it up on the internet. Maths. She had graduated with a degree in physics from Leeds. The building where she'd been found the day before was a shuttered chemical plant. It still belonged to a huge pharmaceutical company but, apart from a handful of security types, there wasn't supposed to be anyone there. The representative he had spoken with at her firm wouldn't give him her assignments. "Data protection," said the nasal voice on the other end of the line. He was told to ask her himself. Another constable, Hesketh, was working her home life, but it was too early to suggest she was anything other than a lucky individual; if being caught in an explosion that flattened a five story industrial site was lucky.

She might not have been his type but Michael could still appreciate just how elegantly beautiful she was. The explosion appeared to have left her entirely unharmed, an initial fear about concussion had passed without incident. Her eyes were huge, almond-shaped and completely symmetrical, her skin was smooth, slightly tanned and radiated a youth his constable, who was younger than Seeker, was already losing to stress and irregular shift patterns. She returned his stare with lazy assessment, leaning back in her chair, arms by her sides, leaving her chest uncovered. Michael's boyfriend, Mark, would have commented sharply that little Miss Seeker was gorgeous and knew it. He thought about his own time in the gym and the dozen little imperfections chance had left him with that nothing but surgery would correct.

If she had undergone surgery it was, without doubt, the finest example of the scalpel at work he had ever seen. Mark was an actor and always said that the truly beautiful had only to turn up and get given stuff. He acidly maintained such beauty ruined them for hard work. She was wearing a corn blue rugby shirt that was a little tight for her, with her hair tied back in a knot that revealed sculpted neck and collar bones.

Michael was rehearsing the conversation he would have with Mark later, the one about the genius on wheels accountant who should be in the movies, when the door behind them opened and Eleanor entered.

"I got you a tea," said Michael. "I hope that's okay."

Stryck plonked the cup on the table and sat down beside him. "I'm constable Stryck. We're sorry we've had to bring you from the hospital, Ms. Seeker. Standard procedure in cases like this." She turned her cup on the table. "We understand that you have been through a terrible ordeal and we're grateful that you're prepared to make a statement."

Michael let the constable lead the interview – woman to woman was considered more appropriate. He resisted the urge to check his phone every couple of minutes; the preliminary report from forensics was due that morning.

"Anything I can do to help," said Seeker. "Please, call me Jayne."

"Jayne," said Stryck, "could you tell us what

happened?"

The look in her eyes changed, but Michael couldn't see her reliving her experience. Instead it was as if she was repeating something rehearsed. Stryck changed her position on the chair next to him and he was pleased to recognise that she too had noticed the change in Jayne's demeanour.

Jayne fingered a heavy locket that hung low on her neck. "Work," she said. "I was there because of my work. I'm an accountant and I was doing a site visit." She picked up speed as she warmed to her subject, the first halting words being replaced by a smooth and assured delivery. "My client required us to look into a certain issue they had with the value of some assets. I'm a subject matter expert in valuing illiquid assets; you know, ABS, derivatives and the like. The asset in this case was a Real Option."

There are those words again, thought Michael. He supposed she was paid much more than him, probably just for knowing what they meant. What he did know was that valuing made up financial instruments didn't need site visits.

"I arrived about 9 am and was being shown around by the site manager." She leaned in conspiratorially and Michael found his eyes drawn to her breasts, which she managed to push forwards without being brazen about it. The move was subtle but the effect undeniable – Michael knew some of his straight friends would have been momentarily lost. "The client's audit implied some business was still ongoing at the site but," she paused, "apart from the security guards the place was derelict."

"You were there investigating fraud?" asked Stryck, sounding as if she didn't quite believe her own words.

"Goodness me, no," said Jayne, sounding offended, "Well, I suppose you could categorise it like that. You are a policewoman. I was there to complete some due diligence before I calculated the option value of the site." She leaned back as if her conclusion was obvious without needing to be said. "Just thinking about the environmental liabilities makes me shudder. The maths says that no option ever has zero value, if it's probable then it's possible and, on that basis, nothing in the future is ever worthless, but this one would have been pretty close to it." She shrugged as if this was of no concern to her while also very bad news for someone else.

"How did you get there?" asked Stryck. Michael's phone buzzed in his pocket. He guessed it was the forensics team. He couldn't read it in front of her but the information would be pertinent.

"I drive a Toyota Prius," said Jayne. "Company car. The details are in my handbag. Do you have my handbag? I'm rather hoping you people collected it while I was unconscious."

Closing the door to the interview room behind him, he saw two officers approaching; the place was getting busy. He thought nothing more of it and checked his messages. He couldn't quite believe his eyes when he saw the preliminary results. Seeker was now their only witness, and only current suspect, to what was being classified as an event that would lead to a Cabinet Office Briefing Room A meeting.

"Excuse me," said a plain-clothed officer, who attempted to push past him and reach for the door.

"Occupied, mate," said Michael, blocking him.

The detective looked puzzled for a moment and then, as if nothing had happened, walked back the way he had come. What the hell? thought Michael, shaking his head in disbelief. His phone buzzed again, like an angry grinding of teeth; the world was about to go mental and Ms Seeker would soon be gone. Rooms with one-way mirrors and people listening to ear buds were her future. Whatever her involvement, Ms. Seeker would also be wanted by people other than her Majesty's government.

He stepped back into the room.

Jayne appeared shaken. She looked up at him with a sharp jerk of her head, frowned and snapped her gaze back to Constable Stryck. "Was he the only one who died?"

"I'm sorry," said Stryck, "we can't confirm that right now."

"At least four others," said Michael. He had decided to be direct, in the hope of getting some sort of result before she was whisked away from him.

Stryck was looking at him as if he had gone mad. Seeker rocked back as if he had punched her in the face. Her hands were now palm down on the table. "God," was all she said.

"When were you last at Manchester Airport?" he asked her.

"Months ago," she said immediately.

"We have found your car," he told her, changing tack.

This time she didn't respond. A hand went to a locket around her neck. Michael noticed, for the first time, that the item was burnt around the clasp, that blackening of melted wire and electrical components he'd managed to create once after attempting to rewire a light switch.

"What's in the locket?" he asked.

"A picture of my mother," said Seeker, hand covering it completely now.

"Would you mind if I had a look?"

The door opened behind them.

Stryck turned in her chair and opened her mouth to kindly ask them to piss off. Michael was forced to look when she said nothing for some moments.

"What?" he said in exasperation and turned around in his seat. Two officers he didn't recognise stood in the door, semi-automatic pistols pointed into the room. They weren't police issue. His chest burned as he looked at the barrel aimed at his face.

The two men moved into the room and closed the door behind them. Michael realised he had stopped breathing. A roar of fear in the silence of the room filled his ears and a thousand thoughts flew through his mind without a single one of them settling. A whizz of motion beside him caused him to dive to his left, his shoulder against the wall.

"No," said Jayne firmly from behind him as the two men shot Michael and Eleanor. The man whose gun was pointed at Michael pulled his trigger but the gun didn't fire. Eleanor wasn't so lucky; a damp bang sounded and she dropped to the ground. She was dreadfully quiet and still.

The man in front of Michael pulled the trigger again but still nothing. The other bastard kicked Stryck's prone body hard. Satisfied that she was done, he turned his gun on Michael. He realised he hadn't moved since that first dive. He could feel time slipping away from him and a desperate urge not to end up like Eleanor, the desire to see Mark again, pulled him into awareness. Michael stood up and leapt at his attacker, throwing a punch over the barrel of the pistol into the man's face. It was poorly thrown but he followed through with his whole body, hoping the other one wouldn't shoot at his mate. More shots rang out and, in the haze of smashing the man's head against the floor until he stopped moving, Michael dimly registered that he wasn't dead.

His attacker was unconscious but alive. He cuffed him and looked around to see Jayne kneeling on the back of the other gunman who was laid flat on his face. She tucked a strand of hair behind her ear and said, "I'm truly sorry, I couldn't stop both of them. Too improbable."

"They would have shot you," he said, trying to reassure her. "Eleanor saved us both." In saying her name he remembered her. "Oh shit." He checked her for the entry wound and realised she was laid on top of it. "Shit, shit, shit." He wanted to cry, to shout.

The door opened with a wrenching crunch. "Everyone freeze!" someone shouted. "On the floor, now!"

Michael looked up, tears pouring down his face. His mate, Andy Clerk, was standing over him with a semi auto pointing down into his face. "Christ, Michael," he said and, shouldering his weapon, knelt down over Eleanor's limp body. Around them people poured into the room, help was called for and hands gently lifted Michael away from his colleague. He didn't remember much more of those moments except the look of sorrow and guilt written across Jayne's face, as if it were all her fault.

Jayne found herself in a much more secure environment; multiple electronically coded doors, guards regularly stationed and enough cctv cameras to make a voyeur wet themselves.

She'd been alone in the observation room for an hour now. She wasn't really alone; on the other side of the mirror people were watching her. The air smelt old, already breathed. The light was dull yet it was still brighter in there than it had been at the police station. This kind of place was limited and dangerous, she felt trapped and the knowledge of someone on the other side of the wall analysing her left Jayne anxious, with a knot of darkness in her stomach. They'd taken her clothes and left her with a paper thin boiler suit and underwear.

Sometime later people came to see her. A man and a woman, both in dark and averagely tailored suits. Marks and Spencer probably, maybe T. M. Lewin. He was tall and angular, she was short with a black bob, pretty in that bland way people who had rich parents often were. They looked tired. She wore no make-up.

They didn't introduce themselves but were polite enough to greet her before starting their interrogation. "Who do you know who might wish to kill you?" she asked.

"I don't know," said Jayne. "I'm an accountant for one of the Big Four." Her voice trembled just enough to seem fearful.

"Who would break into a police station dressed as police officers, shoot a constable and try to kidnap you?" he asked.

"Aren't I entitled to a lawyer?" she asked.

"Do you need one?" countered the woman.

"I don't know," said Jayne. "Do I? Would it help? Two men were sent to kill me, enemies of the ideas I aspire to, and they walked right in here as if they owned the place. Forget the lawyer; can you help me?"

"How do you calculate a Real Option?" he asked, ignoring her.

She laughed bitterly. "You think that asking me that will blow my cover? Fine, get me some paper. Do either of you know what ten percent of one hundred is because unless you've actually got degree level statistics under your belt you're wasting our time."

"So you admit you have a cover," said the woman intently.

Jayne sighed and rubbed her eyes with the fingers of one hand. "What is wrong with you people? I was giving a witness statement when those maniacs arrived. That poor woman died saving my life, but the first people they shot at were the police officers. They didn't seem to care that I was in the room."

Mr Angular shared a brief look with Ms. Bland. "We know about Manchester."

"What?"

"We have the footage of you from Manchester," he said.

"Plus four dead bodies found after an explosion there yesterday which occurred at the same time you were surviving Thames Haven," she said.

"I'm sorry," said Jayne, "are you trying suggest that I was in two places at once? That surviving an explosion is a crime?"

Michael resented having the two men in black muscle in on his case. He found it hard to accept the evidence SIS had presented him with but was glad to still be in the loop. As a former specialist, they'd decided he was on the need to know list. Either that or losing one of his better officers that morning gave him a sympathy vote.

Whatever the truth, they weren't going to get at her like this. If she was just a clever accountant then they were frightening her with patently absurd nonsense. If, somehow, there was any truth to what they were saying then their questions hardly qualified as worthy of amateur hour. He turned to their team leader, a detective inspector by the name of Simmons. "Can I speak to them?"

Simmons nodded and showed him the thin microphone to speak into.

"Look, you two," said Michael, "even if she does admit to being in two places at once, where does that leave you? With a plot out of Star Trek? Real people have died over this; remember your training. Back to basics; treat her like she might be an innocent victim in all this bloody lunacy."

They started over. Jayne didn't understand why they suddenly supposed they should introduce themselves. Mia Holmes and William Moynihan. When had she last been to Manchester? Why was she at the site in Thames Haven?

Jayne relaxed a little. She felt like a person again; a tired person, but human at least. Eventually, some hours later, they started to circle in on the points where Stryck and Lakshmi had also focussed.

"We found your car," said Mia. "How did you get from Manchester Airport to London without it?"

Jayne rubbed at the untanned ring of skin on her finger where her jewellery had once been before they'd taken it. "I was with my colleague, Dennis. He was with me on site."

"We thought you were alone?" they said.

"He was standing next to me when…" She didn't finish.

They heard irritated tutting in their ear buds. "Your evidence says there was no explosive centre at the Thames Haven site. That the particles and accelerant literally originated out of thin air, but that they share identical molecular markers as the explosion at Manchester Airport. Ask her about where they were standing, remind her that there was no live gas, no electrics. Ask her if she's ever worked in Manchester. Think or be replaced."

"Can you think how an explosion could happen out of thin air?" asked Moynihan.

"Dickens wrote about spontaneous combustion," Jayne said flippantly before stopping. She gave the pretence of thinking hard, playing with her hands and pursing her lips. "Nagel says there are two types of truth. External and Internal."

"Subjective and Objective," said Mai helpfully.

"No. Nothing of the sort. As far as physics is concerned, true is true."

"I don't understand," said Moynihan.

"The universe is all connected, right? Basic physics. Entangled particles are just a special case, a type of mathematical sleight of hand that distils the complexity of reality down to something manageable." She pushed her bottom lip out. "Have you ever thought how, in creating these 'special cases', they actually end up confusing the rest of us more? Anyway. Add to the connectedness that everything is up for grabs until it's decided. Then there are many actual truths, sets of truth if you want to borrow from number theory. That is External truth. Internal truth is the reality that happens somewhen, somewhere, that you create when you are in it. Any of the possibilities in the set could have been true, in fact they are true, except that when one of them happens then only that is true and the truth is that the others are not true. That is the Internal truth."

"I still don't get it," said Moynihan while Holmes sat silently. Jayne supposed that before electronic surveillance they would have taken notes. Instead they now recorded every word she said.

She sighed. "There is the view from nowhere and the

view from now here." She folded her arms and smiled wryly. Michael, from the other room, felt as if, all of a sudden, they were the ones under observation. "Let me tell you a story and see if you understand after that. There was once a girl who was lucky. Except the people she grew up with didn't believe in luck, they believed in mathematics. They taught her that if it was probable it was possible. They showed her how to control truth as I've just described it. She could pull truths from nowhere into the now here. When she could be trusted to be consistent they gave her a locket. They never said where the locket came from or who had made it, but showed her that she could use it to handle more than one true version of the world at a time, using it to hold them in tension. She could create entangled worlds and when she was ready, at a time of her choosing, she could choose the one she wanted, or needed, to be true for her.

"Imagine that this girl worked to change the world in ways that suited her and the people she grew up with. One day she found herself in Manchester, dealing with some very bad people. They had an explosive device and had managed to smuggle it flight-side at the airport. She found them and, having prepared another version of the world in which she was in London before she confronted them, pulled the explosion into that other truth she had prepared. Now the probability she had prepared was very slight, but it seemed the safest way to reduce the threat they represented. Unfortunately people died no matter what path through the probability landscape, sorry, possible outcome, she chose."

Silence followed in her wake until Michael prodded his two confused interviewers. "That doesn't explain anything."

As if he'd cleared the mist, they challenged her on her story.

"Okay, I'll try it another way," said Jayne, fingering her locket.

How did she keep that? wondered Michael. Standard procedure should have seen the locket removed along with her rings.

"Suppose this girl wants to leave a place where she is closely guarded and watched. It might go like this: outside this room stands a guard. That guard could do a number of things. He could stay there, he could walk away. He could enter the room. Beyond the obvious is the minor; he could play with his hair, pick his nose or think of his girlfriend rather than his wife. He might remember a lost lover or choose to think of yesterday's football game. All of these are true. All of them happen. They are the view from nowhere.

"However, the girl can choose the possibility that for some reason he opens the door, round chambered and safety off, comes in, trips and inadvertently shoots at the one way mirror. While he does this, she uses the confusion to run. Throughout the complex cctv starts to malfunction as circuit boards choose that moment to fail, or fuses suddenly blow. Somewhere a rat nibbles through a wire and shuts off another. While the surveillance fails more guards are inexplicably, and completely out of character for them, leaving doors open, jammed with fire extinguishers. ID passes are dropped while they hurry somewhere else. The girl doesn't quite know what possibility she'll find until she happens upon it but years of practice help her find her way. She may take a wrong turn, and occasionally someone sees her and calls out, but she's running and in most of the view from nowhere she couldn't possibly be free and running down the corridor, so people ignore what they can't accept as possible. Before the base can be locked down she's in the car park and it just so happens that someone dropped their car keys that morning. She jumps in their car and is gone. She doesn't, indeed can't, use her locket because diverting the explosion damaged it. That doesn't matter. She has made it the view from now here."

In the observation room Simmons laughed. "My, she's good."

"It explains everything," said Michael as he worked

through the timeline of her story.

"Don't be daft," said Simmons.

Jayne looked over the heads of Holmes and Moynihan, "It would all start with her tucking a strand of hair behind her ear and apologising for the death of Constable Stryck."

"Nice story," said Mia wearily.

Jayne looked her in the eyes, "I am truly sorry for Stryck's death. She saved my life and I won't forget her. I cannot help you identify the men who attacked us but, I will find them." Seeker put an errant strand of hair behind her ear.

"Stop her!" Michael shouted into the microphone.

The door to the interview room swung open, the guard stepped in and tripped over his untied shoe lace. The barrel of his sub machine gun veered toward the mirror as he fell.

The Girl With No Face

John Llewellyn Probert

She was beautiful, standing there on my doorstep.

She was soaked from the pouring rain, the black hair that came down to just below her chin plastered in rat-tails to the flawless skin of her heart-shaped face. The strands were so wet the howling wind had been denied the opportunity to arrange them to its own liking, not that she would have been any less appealing as a result of even its most violent efforts.

It was not because of her beauty that I hesitated in the doorway of my own house, having answered the insistent hammering that had come in the minutes approaching midnight and which had stirred me from my research. It was not because of those hazel-gold eyes, so appealing in their silent pleading. Nor because of the tiny pink tongue that darted from between her full lips for a split second. Despite her efforts tiny dots of rain water still glistened just beneath her nose. No, it was not because of any of these reasons.

It was because of the gun she was pointing at me.

"Are you Justin Kelland, the plastic surgeon?" Her honeyed tones augmented her already exquisite perfection. She was obviously either the product of good breeding, or some very expensive elocution lessons. Or possibly both.

My gaze dropped to the pistol before returning to her face. For a moment I considered denying my identity. Then I remembered the brass plate on the gatepost half a mile back down the drive. However she had managed to get up here (I could see no vehicle) it was likely she had checked first to ensure she would be pointing her gun at the right person.

"I am," I replied, my brow creasing. "But I'm not in the habit of accepting guests this late at night."

She pushed past me into the entrance hall, brandishing the weapon to ensure I would step back.

"That's all right, Dr Kelland," she said. "I'm not exactly what you'd call a guest, anyway." With a sweeping glance she took in the walls panelled in cherry wood, the paintings that I had picked up at auction for a small fortune, and the suit of armour in the corner that had been a gift from an eccentric friend. "Very nice," she said, before gesturing to the broad staircase. "Who else is here with you?"

I shook my head. "No one," I replied. "I've lived alone since my wife died a year ago."

She nodded as she looked around, all the while keeping the gun trained on me. "You could still have someone here, though," she said. "Children... servants... lovers."

"We had no children to speak of," I said, "and the servants live in the village. I have no need of them during the nighttime. As for lovers..." I spread my hands. "My research takes up all my time, now."

She held up her left hand for a moment, as if she thought she had heard something. Then she regarded me with those beautiful eyes once more.

"Good," she said. "You have a lovely house here, doctor. I'm assuming there's somewhere we can speak that's more comfortable than your hallway?"

I gestured to a closed door on my right. "Perhaps my study might suit your needs?"

She raised the gun. Whether her hand was shaking from fear or the cold I couldn't tell, although I was keen to find out. "That should be fine," she said. "You go first."

My study is large, comfortable, and lined with books, many of them of a surgical nature. I switched on the light and made to usher the young lady in, but she still insisted I go in front of her. My heavy oak desk is on the far right of the room, facing the window. There is only the one chair.

I crouched near the fireplace, which is located opposite the door, and lit the gas jet. The flame came to life with a roar. "Perhaps you might like to stand here," I said.

The girl stood with her back to the fire and shivered. She pointed to the chair.

"You may as well take a seat," she said. "We're going to be here for a while." She must have read my mind, or seen me regarding the gun still gripped in those tiny chilled fingers, because she felt moved to add, "and don't think about overpowering me. I've dealt with men stronger and more determined than you in my time, and I can promise you, they were the ones who came off worse. So please dispense with any thoughts of turning the tables on me because I know how to use this. It would be the end of your career if you were to receive a bullet through the palm, and neither of us wants that."

She was certainly convincing. In fact her confidence seeming to be growing as she dried off. Any misconceptions I might have harboured about this young lady being meek and helpless were quickly fading. Her arrival at my house was clearly no accident. I suspected the lateness of the hour was deliberate, as well. I took care to place the photograph of my wife that I keep on my desk face down. I had no wish for her to be witness to the nefarious proceedings that were undoubtedly to follow. Then I turned my desk chair round and settled into the red leather upholstery, determined to make myself as comfortable as possible while I was being threatened.

A crack of thunder sounded outside. "I guess you're wondering why I'm here," she said.

"It has crossed my mind," I replied, "although right now I'm far more interested in learning your name."

She laughed at that. I don't think I have ever heard anything quite so mirthless or so empty. However young she looked, that sound made me realise she was older than I had thought. Older, and with the kind of hardened cynicism that only comes to those who have had enough bad experiences to conclude that life is not on their side.

"To be honest, doctor," she said, turning toward me so she could dry the rest of herself, "I've had so many names over the years I've almost forgotten my real one. Not that I would tell it to you, anyway."

I clasped my hands in my lap and crossed my legs, determined to gain the upper hand in the conversation. "Well I have to call you something," I said, calmly, "and I would prefer if it wasn't 'you there' or 'rude girl with a gun', which is all I can think of calling you at the moment."

I knew I was taking a chance saying something like that, but this was my house, and I was still feeling somewhat incensed at this woman's intrusion. I admit to being relieved, however, when she glanced heavenwards and thought for a moment.

"Fair enough, doctor," she said. "You can call me... Angela."

"Very well," I smiled, "Angela. So what has brought you through the pouring rain in the middle of the night to come and see me, Angela?"

She turned her back to the fire again, changed the gun to her left hand and shook the raindrops from her right. "A gentleman who gets to the point. I like that," she said. "I like that very much."

"It's past midnight and I would like to get to bed," I said, leaning forward a little. "Nevertheless, you have aroused my interest. You must need something very badly to be here under such circumstances, and I cannot believe that it's just money."

"Oh, I have plenty of money, doctor," Angela said. "The problem is, I'm not going to get the chance to enjoy any of it if you don't help me."

"Let me guess." It was all starting to become clear. "You have procured for yourself a considerable sum of money by illegal means, but you were seen in the act. Would I be correct so far?" Angela nodded. "And as well as that, you were witnessed doing something so appalling that you need the services of a plastic surgeon to alter your appearance. Otherwise it's life imprisonment for sure."

"I killed a policeman," she said. The gun was down by her side, now. "He'd shot my partner... my lover, actually, and before I knew what was happening I'd fired back. The cop didn't have a chance."

"And therefore neither will you once the authorities catch up with you," I said, rubbing my hands. It was chilly in the room despite the fire. "I presume I'm right?"

The girl took a step forward, that pleading look in her eyes again, the one that for all I knew had tricked a hundred men before me. "I just need you to change my looks a little," she said. "Just enough that I can't be matched up with any eyewitness accounts. You can do that, can't you? And I'll pay. My car's hidden just off your driveway. The money's still in the boot. If you help me I can make sure we both come out of this rich."

From my comfortable antique leather chair I raised my hands and looked around me. "Do I look as if I need your money?" I said.

Angela gave me a cold look. "I'm sure you could use a little more, doctor."

I dropped the warmth from my tones in response. "Perhaps," I said, "although there are other things I value more."

"Like your life, you mean?" She raised the gun. "Don't think I won't use this, doctor. After all, I have killed already today. I might just be getting the taste for it."

I waved away her threat. "I can see the only way I'm going to be able to get rid of you is to accede to your wishes. But before I can tell you how much I can change your face, I need to have a good look at it."

She took two steps forward, and kneeled in front of

me.

"No, no no," I was already getting to my feet. "The light in here is terrible. You'll have to come to my operating theatre."

For the first time I saw real fear in her eyes, and dare I say it gave me a twinge of pleasure.

"You have an operating theatre here?"

I nodded. "Of course. For my richest private patients who prefer not to attend a hospital. I can't do everything up there, but it's extensively equipped for the performing of a number of procedures." I held out my hand. "So if you would be kind enough to accompany me? And for goodness' sake put that gun away. I'm sure you can get to it quickly enough should the need arise. Which it isn't going to."

She seemed happy with that, tucking the pistol into the back of her black skirt as she got to her feet with my assistance.

We left the study and ascended the broad staircase to the first floor.

"Which one is the operating theatre?" Angela asked, viewing the heavy oak doors that led off the corridor, two on either side.

"None," I replied. "These are bedrooms. My place of work is further up."

A narrower staircase took us up to the next level. I could feel Angela shivering beside me as I slid the key into the locked door.

People are always impressed by my operating theatre, and the young lady with me was no exception. She followed me inside, and, once I had switched on the main lights, it was all she could do not to stare open-mouthed at what lay before her.

"When I was younger I always dreamed of having my own place of work," I explained. "Preferably at the top of a large country house. The glass ceiling allows me to operate using daylight when the sun is shining, but I had the floodlights installed for when the weather turns gloomy."

"Or when you have to operate at night," Angela breathed, still taking in the ice-white walls and the glass cabinets of instruments that gleamed silver in the artificial light.

And, of course, the operating table.

"If you'd like to jump up," I said, gesturing to it, "you'll find it's extremely comfortable. Then I can have a really good look at you."

She drew back from my outstretched hand. "You're not going to do anything right away, are you?" she said.

"Goodness me, no!" I replied. "I'll examine you now, explain what I think I can do, and then it will be up to you to decide if you wish to proceed."

Once she was on the table, a bright light on her upturned face, I noticed something very interesting.

"You've had plastic surgery before." I was tracing the fine scar that had been expertly concealed behind her left ear.

"Did I say I hadn't?" Angela replied.

"It would have been worth pointing out." I examined her face more closely with a magnifying glass. "Your eyelids have been tightened, your nose has been altered, and your cheekbones have undergone a serious amount of reconstruction."

"It took him several hours," she said as I checked beneath her chin. Her hyoid bone had been shortened as well.

"You mean David Harcourt?" I checked her face for a reaction and was suitably rewarded. "I should be able to recognise his work." I shone a torch on her brow and checked how slack her scalp was. "After all, I trained him."

Satisfied that I now knew what I had to work with, I took a step back.

"Now," I said, "seeing as this isn't the first time you've

had plastic surgery I'm guessing that neither is this the first time you've needed someone to get you out of trouble."

The gun was pointing at me again as Angela gave me a very becoming pout.

"So this isn't the first time I've been a bad girl," she said. "But that was just over a year ago and my skin should be back to its youthful pliable self by now. I've certainly been using moisturiser like it's going out of style."

"About a year ago?" I rubbed my chin, deep in thought. I gave the girl's face one last check, conscious of the gun pressing against my side as I did so, and then I nodded.

"I can certainly do something for you," I said. "By the time I'm finished I can guarantee you'll look different."

Angela visibly relaxed. "Thank God," she said. "Please do whatever you can. I don't need to be an oil painting, I just need to look different to this."

"Of course." I wheeled over a canister of nitrous oxide and was about to apply the face mask when she stopped me.

"Oh no, doctor," she said. "You're not putting me out."

"It's just to dull the pain," I said, "you won't be able to keep still without it."

Angela was having none of it. "I'm staying awake for this. You can use local anaesthetic, just like Harcourt did."

"It will still hurt," I said. "Quite a lot."

"Then I'll have to grin and bear it quite a lot, won't I?" she said.

"You will," I said, too tired to argue as I filled a syringe and fitted a large needle.

To give Angela her due, she only screamed twice, but by the time her face was being bandaged she had passed out. I left her on the operating table to sleep as I went downstairs. There were things I needed to tend to.

The police called round early the next morning. Before retiring for the night I had carried Angela from the operating table to the small recovery room I have adjacent to my theatre. She was still sound asleep and, following the sedative I had administered, I knew she would remain so for several hours yet. I had also taken the opportunity to divest her of her firearm and lock the door. Rather than being part of her plan, she was now part of mine.

The constable who knocked on my door was a young fresh-faced chap called Tate. Once he had confirmed my identity his sergeant, the older and considerably more world-weary Sergeant Blaydon took over.

"We're very sorry to bother you, Dr Kelland," he said. "But we're just checking door to door to see if anyone's seen or heard anything strange hereabouts in the last twelve hours or so."

I shook my head. "I'm afraid I've been asleep for most of that, sergeant," I said, not needing to fake the yawn that came unbidden right at that moment. "What's the matter?"

The two policemen exchanged glances.

"We've been given to understand that a dangerous criminal may be at large, sir," said Blaydon eventually. "They were involved in a robbery, and were last seen headed this way. We also believe them to be armed."

"Oh my goodness." I did my best to look shocked. "What does this man look like?"

"It's not a man sir," said Blaydon, showing me a picture of someone who now hardly resembled the girl upstairs in my recovery room. "Have you by any chance seen this woman?"

I made a show of examining the photograph carefully before shaking my head.

"We're also asking everyone to make sure their houses are secure as we believe she may still be in the area, sir," said Tate.

"What gives you that idea?" I was curious to learn what else they might know.

"There was a murder in Pensham village last night sir,"

said Blaydon. "Sharon Francis, on her way home from tending bar at The Coach and Horses."

"Someone on foot did her in a right treat," said Tate before his superior could stop him. "She was almost unrecognisable when we found her."

"The footprints double back this way, sir," said Blaydon, "which is why we're combing the area. You will be careful won't you, sir?"

"I certainly will, sergeant," I said. "And thank you. I promise to let you know the moment I see anything suspicious."

"Thank you sir," said Tate. "We'll leave you to your business now."

And what very important business it was. Once the police had left, I made my way down to the cellar to ensure that all was prepared. There was a certain amount of excitement at this, and it was all I could do to keep calm. Eventually, though, everything was ready. I checked my watch.

She should be waking up around now, I thought.

My calculations were almost exact. Within five minutes of my arriving at Angela's bedside she was stirring into groggy wakefulness. She looked at me through the slit I had left in the bandages for her eyes and mumbled something.

"You'll have to wait until I remove these before I can hear you," I explained, taking out a pair of scissors and commencing to snip at the pieces of tape tethering the soft material.

I had to keep pushing her hands away as she tried to assist me. It was important that the dressings were taken down in a specific way, and I did not want her ruining all my work of the previous night.

Eventually, we found ourselves face to face.

"Be careful about speaking," I warned as she tried to talk, "or indeed making any violent movement. I've used almost invisible sutures, but there's still a reasonable amount of swelling that will take a while to settle down."

She reached tentative fingertips to her face.

"None of that either," I said, pushing her hands back down to her sides. "No poking or prodding until doctor says – understand?"

"Can I see?" Her voice was a whisper filtered through swollen lips.

"Of course," I took the hand mirror from my pocket and held it up to her face. "What do you think?"

I gave her a moment to take everything in before continuing.

"You'll notice how I've fleshed out the cheekbones and made your face much rounder overall," I said. "I've recessed the chin, lowered your eyebrows slightly and brought them closer together. You're not as attractive as you once were, I'll admit, but you also look very different. Which, I am sure you will agree, was the point of the endeavour."

The woman who looked nothing like she had when she arrived last night stared at her reflection. A single tear welled up in one eye.

"That's because of the disfiguring scar isn't it? The gouge that runs through your right eyebrow, down your cheek and to the corner of your mouth? In time you'll come to thank me for it, you know. Instead of being a beautiful girl on the run you are now the proud owner of what the police call a Distinguishing Feature." I sat back a little to behold my handiwork. "No one is looking for someone like you," I said. "You have effectively escaped your pursuers – congratulations!"

Angela did not seem quite so delighted with the result. She reached out with shaking hands and gripped my shoulders.

"Change... it... back," she said.

"Change it?" I tutted. "Oh my goodness me, no. I can't do that. To do even more plastic surgery now, on top of all that you've had, both past and present, would be risky. Very risky indeed. Plus you need to rest, and the equipment I need for such radical restructuring is kept downstairs in a room I reserve for my very special complex cases."

"I don't care," she mumbled, the tears flowing freely now. "I'll take my chances. Change it back."

I pretended to consider this for a moment, before nodding.

"I'm afraid I'll have to double my fee," I said, as gently as possible.

It was only at that point that she remembered the gun.

"It's no good looking for that dangerous thing," I said. "I've put it well out of harm's way so nothing silly happens. Do you feel strong enough to walk?"

She did, which was just as well as it would have been a long way to carry her. I helped her down the narrow steps to the first floor, and then she was able to descend the broad staircase to the ground by herself. She frowned as I opened a heavy oak door beneath the staircase, beyond which lay blackness.

"I'm sorry," I explained, "when I said the room is downstairs I meant under the house. There was no room up here for such an elaborate setup and so I had the old wine cellars converted." I flicked a switch to reveal a plushly carpeted stairwell leading down. "Come on," I said, betraying a sense of irritation, "it's time to get this sorted out."

Angela tentatively followed me. The brow of her newly disfigured face was creased with concern and it was causing some degree of bleeding from the left lateral edge. I didn't feel it was worth mentioning.

At the bottom we came to another door, which I had to unlock with a heavy iron key. It swung inwards, the room beyond swallowed by blackness.

"Step inside," I said matter-of-factly, "and I'll find the light switch."

Whether or not she trusted me I have no idea, but I had counted on her being far too desperate to turn back now, and I was right. Angela took a step inside, and then another, as I followed her in.

"The floor's made of stone," she managed to say.

"Of course it is," I replied as I lit the oil lamp I had left inside the door. "It makes it easier to clean."

The glow from the lamp revealed little, but it was enough for her to see the dripping stone walls, flickering with shadows cast by the flame. She took a step back and her foot slid on the straw that had been scattered there.

"What is this?" she said.

"Ah, now," I said, holding the lamp up higher and ignoring, for the moment, the scuffling noise from behind her, "in order to explain that I need to show you something."

It was then that I took the photograph from my pocket, the one of my poor dead wife that I had seen fit to conceal when Angela had barged her way into my study.

"Do you recognise her?" I said.

Angela peered at the picture.

"It's me," she said before correcting herself. "It's my face."

I shook my head. "It is not you," I said. "This is my wife. She was killed in an accident a year ago by a hit and run driver. The police said the car was being used to escape the scene of a crime. She didn't die straight away, and she was left with that terrible facial scar I've seen fit to give you as well. Now I'm not saying you were involved, although fate sometimes has an interesting way of causing such coincidences to occur. Nevertheless, if she was not killed by you, she was killed by someone like you. That is good enough for me." There was a noise like a chain being rattled somewhere behind us, accompanied by the dull grunt of a tethered animal. "And," I said after an appropriate pause, "I'm sure it will be good enough for our son Raymond as well."

Angela tried to get past me but by now I had dropped the photograph and the gun was in its place. "I'm afraid you can't leave," I said. "You see, when I said we had no children to speak of, it's only because Raymond was our guilty little secret. The boy we could tell no one about or he would have been taken away from us. His mother would never have permitted that. She loved him too much. And he loved her."

There was a louder grunt from behind Angela, but I kept the gun trained on her and she didn't move.

"I've often thought that all he needs to calm him down is to have someone to replace her," I explained. "Other women just don't seem to make him happy. I've been researching it extensively. I tried again yesterday, but he didn't like the poor girl I brought him from the village at all. So when you turned up last night, right after I'd taken care of disposing of her body, how could I not take advantage of the opportunity to give him back his mother?" I took two steps back. Angela tried to follow, but I fired a shot close to her foot, just to show I meant business.

"I'll leave you the lamp so you can acquainted," I said, "and I'll be back at lunchtime to see how the two of you are getting on. All he wants is a cuddle or two. And if he's naughty just use your 'don't mess with me' voice. The one you used on me last night. It should work like a charm."

I closed and locked the door to the sound of muffled grunts and a long, drawn-out scream. That wasn't how to behave in front of my son. That wasn't the way at all.

"Be calm but firm!" I called through the door, only to be rewarded with silence. Perhaps it was because she was making friends with him. I would give them a few hours together before coming back to check how things were going. I hoped that this time he would at least leave her face alone – it always seemed to be the part of a girl that fascinated him the most.

High Church

Jonathan Oliver

Madeleine was considering a second gin and tonic when a man in a garish Christmas jumper sat himself on the stool beside her. The plastic reindeer's nose on his chest lit up and the relevant ditty issued from somewhere within the cable knit.

"That's unusual," she said.

"Yes, isn't it? I'm Richard. Can I buy you a drink?"

"I wouldn't say no to another G&T."

When the barman placed the drinks before them, Richard fanned his face theatrically and said, "Rather warm in here, isn't it? Think I'll just take this off."

"Now that its desired effect has been achieved, you mean?"

He blushed. "Something like that."

Madeleine waited until he'd struggled out of his novelty jumper before she put down her drink.

"You know," she said, "you're right. It is a bit muggy in here."

And she removed her own jumper, folding it neatly on the bar beside her.

She looked up to see Richard's drink hovering before his lips, his eyes fixed on the dog collar now revealed at her neck.

"Cheers," Madeleine said, clinking her glass against Richard's, his drink slopping over his frozen hand.

"So," she continued, "are you looking forward to Christmas?"

"Erm... yes, that is..."

"Perhaps we'll see you in church?"

"Is that...?" Richard patted his pocket and retrieved a mobile phone. "Yes... I think it was. Sorry, I just have to..."

He hurried away from the bar, his phone glued to his ear, his face burning.

Madeleine raised her drink to his back and smiled.

Being a single woman could be tricky at times, but being a single woman vicar presented its own set of challenges.

"Can I get you another, vicar?" The barman said as he whisked away her empty glass.

"No, I think that's enough sinning for one evening and, beside, work in the morning and all that."

"Work? It's Sunday tomorrow is it?"

"Oh, ha ha."

Outside *The Who'd Ha Thought It* she waited a good five minutes before a break in the traffic allowed her to cross the road. It took all of her Christian resolve not to raise her middle finger at the Mini which came dangerously close to clipping her.

The dark bulk of the vicarage loomed at Madeleine as she made her way down the rutted drive. She'd heard of newly appointed clergy who had been placed in quaint country cottages with ivy climbing the walls and thatch covering the eaves. She even knew of one vicar whose job came with a five bedroom Georgian terrace complete with underground garage and live-in housekeeper. Though Madeleine loved her parish dearly, in terms of housing she hadn't been quite as lucky as some of her fellow ministers.

The vicarage may have been built in the brutalist style – Madeleine wasn't sure, not being *aux fait* with architectural terms. Either way, it had probably seemed like a good idea in the sixties, but now it just screamed eyesore. She had requested some modernisation from the parish office, but was, for now, stuck with living in the past with temperamental central-heating and rising damp.

That evening, after trying to hear the radio over the knocking of water pipes, she was about to turn in for the night when the phone rang.

"Madeleine? It's Peter Barkely at All Saints. Listen, I wouldn't usually ask this, only I can't find any other clergy to cover for me. Anyway, long story short, Grahame Staines is on his way out."

"Grahame Staines?"

"Ah, yes. Sorry, I forgot how new you are. Grahame was the last but one incumbent of St Mark's. He'd still be there, haunting the place, if the parish hadn't removed him on grounds of ill health. Anyway, his carer just called to say that he's not going to last the night, so I need you to be there to attend to him."

"And you can't because...?"

"I'm in Antigua until next week."

"Lovely. I'm sure that it's very nice this time of year."

"Oh, it's not a holiday. No, it's a conference on pastoral care."

"In Antigua?"

"Yes... anyway, would you be a love and do this one favour for me?"

Be a love? Who does he bloody think... Christian thoughts, Madeleine. Christian thoughts.

"Of course. Let me know the address and I'll head over now."

"Thank you so much. I owe you one."

"Just get me on that conference next year, eh?"

Lake View House looked out not upon a lake but a landfill site on one side and a busy road on the other; not a place one would choose to die in. The high-rise should have been pulled down years ago but, for reasons Madeleine didn't entirely understand, had recently achieved listed status.

Inside, the lifts were out – "Of course, why wouldn't they be?" Madeleine mumbled to herself – and Peter had told her that Grahame Staines lived on the fourteenth floor.

She started up the poorly lit stairwell – Bible in her right hand, small leather satchel in her left – fervently hoping that the Reverend Peter Barkely was having a lovely time in Antigua, and not at all wishing a bizarre accident befall him involving the pointy end of a cocktail umbrella.

By the eighth floor she was seriously out of breath, and so not at all prepared for the sight that came lumbering down the stairs towards her.

The Rottweiler stopped. Its tongue lolled and its tail wagged, and for a moment Madeleine thought that she was going to be okay. But when she held out her hand and said "Hey there. And what's your name?" a growl issued from deep in the dog's throat, sending a jolt of fear lancing through her.

Madeleine knew that if she turned and fled the dog would be on her before she could reach the next landing, and trying to edge past the beast and continue on her way was clearly not an option. Realising that she may well die before she could get to the dying, she did the only thing she could.

The Bible was a family heirloom, originally belonging to her great-grandmother on her mother's side. Its pages were edged with gold leaf and the cover was red aromatic leather stretched over wooden boards. When the book connected with the dog's jaw there was a sickening *crack* that at first made Madeleine worry about the integrity of the Bible, and then made her hope that she hadn't injured the dog too badly.

The Rottweiler dropped, the stink of dog briefly filling her nostrils as it tumbled past her, its flank connecting with a meaty thud on the landing railing below.

Madeleine stood frozen to the spot, wracked with guilt at the thought that she may have killed the dog. But then its hind legs twitched, its eyes opened, and it growled.

A frenzied barking followed her as she fled, and

Madeleine was terrified that the dog would be on her in seconds before a cry of "Rommel, you cunt! Get the fuck in here" silenced the animal. There was the scuffle of claws on concrete, a door slamming, and then silence. She breathed a sigh of relief.

Outside 14b she tried to regain some of her former composure, wiping her brow with her stole and straightening her jacket. When she knocked, the door was answered by a young man with a stethoscope around his neck and a name badge that read: Stu.

"Oh, hi. I'm Madeleine Drew." Stu didn't respond and seemed to be considering whether to close the door in her face, perhaps thinking that she was trying to sell something. "You know, the vicar?"

"Oh, right! Right, sorry." Stu laughed. "I wasn't expecting..."

"A woman?"

"I was going to say someone so young."

"Well, thank you, Stu. Is Grahame...?"

"Still with us? Just. Follow me."

This wasn't the first death bed that Madeleine had attended, but it was perhaps the most Spartan. There was nothing in the room beyond the bed on which the elderly priest lay and a cabinet, on top of which stood a lamp and a glass of water. Madeleine thought that in one's last moments, a person would want to be surrounded by family, or at least mementos of familial love – pictures and the like – but the room was virtually bare.

As his carer had said, Grahame Staines clearly didn't have long. Each uneven breath rattled as it was dragged in and out, and the shadows were deeply pooled in the hollows of his face.

"Would you like me to leave you alone with him?" Stu said, nervously fingering his stethoscope.

"No, that's fine, Stu. You can stay."

Madeleine placed her Bible on the bedside cabinet and

took a small vial of oil from her satchel.

"Grahame, as you are coming to this part of your journey, may I pray with you for God's blessing?"

The rattling wheeze stopped abruptly and Madeleine thought that he had gone before she had even begun, but then the priest's eyes briefly fluttered open and the wheezing began again.

"I'd just go ahead if I were you, vicar." Stu said.

Madeleine dipped her index finger into the oil and then made the sign of the cross on Grahame's forehead.

"Grahame, receive the sign of the cross, the mark of your baptism, the sign of your salvation. May God who is faithful bless you and–"

A clawed hand shot up from the bed clothes and clamped painfully around her wrist. The elderly priest's eyes snapped open, and this time they stayed open.

"A... ah..." he gasped, his head straining above the pillow.

Ignoring the trickle of oil running beneath the sleeve of her shirt, Madeleine leaned in close.

"Yes, Grahame? Is there something you would like to say?"

"*A woman!*" The two words were shouted directly into her face.

Stu hurried to the bedside and tried to gently remove the priest's hand from Madeleine's wrist, but she was held fast.

"Now, Mr Staines. We gain nothing from being agitated, do we?" Stu said.

"*They sent... a woman?*"

The water glass on the bedside table jumped a short distance into the air and then exploded. Madeleine was only vaguely aware of the shards peppering her face. All of her awareness was on the pain of the priest's fingers digging into her. It was as though his grip were sinking deep into her flesh. She thought that she smelled incense burning, though she hadn't brought any with her.

"L-lord... now let your servant depart in peace, a-according to your..."

But she got no further, for a great darkness rose up from the bed and took her.

Peter Barkely blew out the candle and, at the same time, the chanting ceased.

He released his grip on the hands he had been holding and uncrossed his legs. As he got to his feet, a sudden cramp gripped his right calf and he hissed in pain.

"You know," he said to those sat within the circle, "all things considered, I really would much rather be in Antigua."

Madeleine came to, jerking back into consciousness so forcefully that she dropped the glass of whisky she had been holding. She watched it roll across the carpet of her study and fetch up against the foot of her desk.

She had no memory of returning to the vicarage. The last thing she could recall was praying over the elderly priest as he thrashed about in his bed. And now, here she was.

Somehow she'd made her way home, somehow she'd poured herself a whisky – a spirit she didn't drink or keep in the house. Madeleine saw the empty Londis bag in the bin and realised that somehow she had also been shopping.

She dialled Peter Barkely's mobile, but there was no reply. She would have called Stu or even Graeme Staines himself, but she hadn't been given either number, so there was no way to check just what had happened.

After a couple of hours spent trawling the internet for the symptoms of a brain tumour, Madeleine realised that she was only making herself more anxious. No doubt exhaustion, job stress and the two gin and tonics she'd consumed earlier had all added to... whatever had happened. For now, she decided to go to bed and call her GP first thing in the morning.

The following two days passed without incident. Madeleine didn't suffer from another 'episode', as Doctor Ewing had called it, and life at the vicarage continued much as it had before. On Friday the local paper ran an obituary of Grahame Staines. The accompanying photo showed a severe looking man with a shock of jet black hair and a piercing gaze. He had apparently been the vicar of St Mark's for six decades – a parish record – and tended to his flock with 'utmost diligence, dedication and fiercely held convictions.' "Sounds like a right barrel of laughs," Madeleine muttered as she threw the paper in the bin.

Six decades, though, that *was* impressive. The Reverend Staines must have made quite the mark on Abbeyfield.

On Sunday she rose early and walked down to the church, breathing deeply of the spring air and admiring the daisies scattered across the vicarage's lawn. Ahead of her, St Mark's was wreathed in a light mist, the headstones in the graveyard seeming to hover before the dark granite of the church.

Madeleine thought that she saw someone pacing her down the hill – perhaps Gavin Nesbitt, the organist, who usually liked to arrive good and early – but when she turned there was nobody there.

Ducking beneath the lichgate, she remembered fragments from the dream she had experienced – something about earth raining down on her upturned face.

Shaking her head clear of the night's phantoms, she used the massive iron key to unlock the double doors of the church porch. She had barely stepped across the threshold when the darkness rose to take her again.

"... a lovely service, vicar. Just lovely. And, pardon my French, but I'm glad that you finally had the balls to say it. Something *does* need to be done about those scroungers and immigrants – expecting free handouts as they pop out yet more children they can't look after. Anyway, keep up the good work."

Madeleine found herself outside her own church, shaking hands with the departing congregation, the sound of the organ echoing through the porch behind her.

Another hand grasped hers. It was Ivy Butler, one of the more senior members of her flock. "Good for you, Madeleine. You know, your sermon reminded me of the good old days of Grahame Staines."

Good Lord, what had she said?

Not all of the people filing past offered their hands, and from the expression on some of the faces a good many would not be returning to St Mark's next Sunday.

Am I going mad?

"Not mad, no."

The voice sounded like it came from directly behind her, a chill breeze insinuating itself into her ear.

"Madeleine," said Patricia Stevens, a young mother who she had shared a bottle of Shiraz with on many an occasion, "I don't know what happened in there, but get help."

"Yes... yes, I will."

Ignoring the rest of the congregation, Madeleine fled back up the hill to the vicarage, where she shut herself in the study.

The whisky glass was still where she had left it, on the floor against her desk, and she had to fight the urge to pick it up and fill it. Instead, she closed her eyes.

"Lord, be with me during this time. Let me get to the heart of the problem and know that you are by my side at all times."

No sooner had she spoken the words of the prayer than the phone rang. It was Paul Green, her curate.

"Madeleine, I must say that I was rather shocked by the content of your sermon."

She wanted to say that she was under a lot of stress, she wanted to tell him that she was seriously worried she may have a brain tumour, but when she opened her mouth, the words that came were not her own.

"It is time, Paul, that we stopped stepping so daintily around the truth. It is time that this modern church of ours stop dressing up scripture to appease the liberal agenda. It is not my job to tell people what they want to hear."

There was a long silence, during which Madeleine railed against the words she had unwittingly spoken, but she was trapped within her own skull, her silent screams echoing in her ears.

"I think, in that case, Madeleine, that I'm going to have to reconsider my position at St. Mark's."

"Yes, I rather think you should."

And before she could command it to do otherwise, her hand had returned the phone to its cradle, ending the call.

For a moment, all that she could do was sit and stare at the phone, her body rigid with shock. Whatever she had said during the sermon, they hadn't been *her* words. And now she had dismissed her curate entirely against her will. It was as though she had been taken over by something, as though she had been...

... No. She didn't want to start using *that* word. It was far too reminiscent of *The Exorcist*, and this was the modern church, this was *her* church.

"No! This church is mine"

The time the voice that came from her lips was most certainly not her own; the cadence of the words was slightly different, but the vehemence behind them, the spiteful tone, could not be mistaken.

"Reverend Staines?"

"Ah... at last you understand."

"Hang on... hang on just a moment." *No no no! This cannot be happening.* "When I prayed over you the other night, when you passed on, did you..."

"Enter you? Yes." And the filthy laugh that came from her lips chilled her to the bone.

"What do you want with me?"

"With you? Nothing. What I want is my church back. What I want is to return my flock to the true path."

"Sorry, *your* church? I hate to break this to you Grahame, but you died. St Marks is *my* church."

"The priesthood is no place for a woman!"

There was a knock on the study door and Madeleine realised that, in her haste, she must have left the front door of the vicarage wide open. Had whoever was standing on the other side heard her conversation? If so, what would they think when the door opened and they found Madeleine alone?

"Come in," she said.

The man who walked into the room was wearing a grey suit, blue shirt and a dog collar. Madeleine didn't recognise the vicar, but she was glad of the clerical company – if anybody could understand her predicament, it would be another priest.

"Can I help you?" she said.

"Madeleine? I'm Paul Barkely. We spoke on the phone the other day."

"Oh... yes. Actually, you have perfect timing. You see, ever since I went to see Reverent Staines, I... wait a moment, aren't you supposed to be in Antigua?"

Peter Barkely walked slowly towards her, his eyes studying her face intently – perhaps he was looking for signs of madness?

"Reverend Staines, are you in there?" he said.

"What? You can't be–" but before Madeleine could finish the sentence her words were stolen from her, and the strange male voice emerged once again.

"Yes, I'm here, Barkely. However, I don't yet seem to have full mastery. This one still has... opinions and some semblance of control."

Peter Barkely sat down and removed his dog collar

before undoing the top button of his shirt. Madeleine could just make out the blue-black stain of a tattoo scrolling up the base of his throat.

"Bugger," he said. "I told them. I said the chant wasn't pitched right. Though, to be fair, the book that you gave us wasn't exactly clear on the details of the ritual."

Madeleine found herself pouring a whisky for the rogue priest and as she handed it to him, he ran his fingers lightly over her hand. "Ah, but such smooth skin, Reverent Staines."

"Shut up! Quite why a woman had to be the vessel—"

Peter Barkely held up his hand, cutting him short.

"You've got your church back, haven't you?"

"But I don't have full control!"

"You will, soon. The new ritual will see to that tonight. In the meantime," Peter Barkely stood, knocking back the whisky and re-securing his dog collar, "hang in there."

Madeleine came to as the last rays of the sun dipped below the roof of St Mark's. On the desk, the flashing light of the answer machine told her that she had twenty-five new messages. She wanted to call everybody back, tell them that she was still here, that what had happened was not her fault, but she realised that she did not have the time do so. Peter Barkely had said that the ritual would be completed tonight.

There was only one thing for it. Madeleine would go over to All Saints and put a stop to this right now while she still had at least some control of her body.

Taking down the parish directory from the shelf above her desk, she looked for the listing for Peter Barkely's church. There was an All Fathers, but no All Saints.

A quick Google search confirmed her fears: whoever Peter Barkely was, he was not a minister in the Church of England. She was, however, surprised to find that a search on the Reverend Grahame Staines threw up a fair amount of information. He was the author of three books – all self-published: *The Hard Truth: Christ's Words as He Actually Meant Them, Marriage: The Tenets of an Institution,* and *Sons of Christ – Daughters of Servitude.* His views were often regarded as 'inflammatory' and 'reactionary' and one theologian even described him as a 'good old-fashioned, hellfire and fury tub thumper; a dying breed and a remnant of an archaic and patriarchal institution'. An enterprising parishioner had even seen fit to transcribe several of his sermons, in which he spent much of his time 'shocked': at the moral laxity of the young, at working mothers, at immigrants and, in particular, homosexuals.

Madeleine looked up as something black and ragged passed by the window. She could feel a presence at her back, a hand resting on her shoulder that felt like it was made of sticks. She blinked and the last of the daylight was gone, the North Star now shining like a promise at the apex of the church spire. She had a sense that silence had just returned to the room, that she had finished a conversation, though she could recall nothing of what had been spoken.

"Right, Reverend Grahame Staines," she said, getting to her feet, pushing the dark whispering to the back of her mind with a burst of mental determination, "that's quite enough of that."

Putting on make-up was something of a challenge with the revenant of a recently deceased Anglican priest standing at one's shoulder. On several occasions Madeleine had felt the Reverend Staines trying to regain control, but she had focused her will and pushed him away. Unfortunately this hadn't stopped him talking to her, or scowling at her in the mirror as she applied mascara.

"And here we see the moral laxity of the modern church," he railed. *"Here we see a priest, a woman priest no less, applying paint to her face so that she looks like nothing more than a common whore."*

"What? I'm hardly tarting myself up, Grahame. Anyway, Margaret Thatcher wore make-up. Are you about to tell me that she was a whore, too?"

The dead vicar had nothing to say to that. Instead, he slammed the front door in her face as she went to leave the vicarage.

Ignoring the outburst, Madeleine made her way across the road, all the while aware of a dark muttering in the back of her mind.

The *Who'd Ha Thought It* was clearly the place to be on a Sunday night. Disco lights sprayed whirling rainbows against windows fogged by condensation. Pop music thudded through the walls of the pub, so loud that Madeleine could feel the vibration of it against her skin.

"Madeleine," one of the door staff acknowledged her with a nod as she entered the pub.

Inside, it was busier than she had ever seen it. The tiny dance floor was packed and the queues at the bar were three deep as people drank as though tomorrow wasn't a Monday. Tinsel brushed her head as she ducked past a low beam to find a place from which she could order a drink.

"You would bring me here? No wonder the reputation of the church is in the pits!"

"You're telling me that you lived opposite a pub and never popped in for a swift pint? No wonder you're such a joyless wa –"

"Madeleine, what can I get you?" The barman stood before her, ignoring the shouts of frustration from some of the other booze-hungry punters.

"Glass of red wine, please, Ted. Bit mad tonight isn't it?"

"Well, Christmas and all that."

"Ah yes. At least the meaning of Christ's birth hasn't been lost on this lot, eh?"

"Well, it's clearly been lost on you!" The dead priest tried to drive the words beyond her lips, but Madeleine covered his utterance with a fit of coughing.

"Nasty cold you've got there, vicar. You should be

tucked up in bed."

"Yes, I should be. There's just something I need to do first."

Securing herself a seat, Madeleine scanned the room, looking for a likely candidate – but many of the men here were either far too young or far too drunk.

When a well-groomed gentleman leant against the bar next to her to order a drink, Reverend Staines took control of Madeleine's legs and she had very nearly marched all the way to the door before she managed an abrupt about-face. She noticed then that she was beginning to draw looks, and not of the sort that she had intended.

On the dance floor in the corner, a woman threw her arms into the air, turning round and round in the circle of men who had gathered to watch her. The scene was obscured by a blast of dry ice and, as it rolled towards her, Madeleine could smell incense. The room darkened and the music slowed, becoming a low sonorous chant. At the bar, a man was using a puddle of spilled bear to sketch strange symbols onto the dark wood.

"The ritual is coming to a head. This will all be over soon, Madeleine. All you have to do is just let go."

Madeleine focused her will and fought her way back into her body just in time to catch the wine glass before it hit the floor. She straightened up to see the door in front of her opening and a familiar face stepping into the fug of perspiration and alcohol.

It was Richard, the man from the other night; he of the novelty jumper and the poor chat-up technique. She grabbed his arm, hoping that the sudden grave-like stench that assaulted them wasn't coming from her.

The colour drained from Richard's face when he recognized her.

"Vicar? I –"

"Richard, I don't have much time to explain but I need you to do something for me."

"Erm, listen. I'm supposed to be meeting –"

"It's for charity and it will only take a second."

Richard smiled, letting his guard down a little. "Yeah, okay."

Madeleine closed her eyes and leaned in close. She allowed the Reverend Staines almost all the way in then; she could feel his foul presence pouring into her like ice-cold water. Her legs were his legs, her arms were his arms, and her lips were his lips.

And so, Madeleine used the last of her will to push those lips up against Richard's in a warm, moist kiss, hoping that the Reverend Grahame Staines could feel everything.

There was a bellow of appalled rage that seemed to go on forever, and then nothing.

"This is the word of God," she said, closing the Bible before returning it to its stand. As she quickly shuffled through her sermon notes, she saw Peter Barkely enter the church and quietly slip into a far pew. There was a look of anticipation on his face, a sick kind of hope.

She adjusted the radio mic clipped to her stole and cleared her throat.

"'You shall love your neighbour as yourself.' It's simple, isn't it? But so many of us seem to forget. And here, we must also remember that neighbour means everyone. *Everyone.*"

Madeleine glanced up and the look of shock and disappointment on Peter Barkely's face filled her with a triumphant joy. Getting up so abruptly that he almost tipped over the pew, he stormed from the church.

She smiled and it took all of her will, all of her Christian resolve, not to call out after him, *"And don't let the church door hit you on the arse on the way out!"*

Valerie

Maura McHugh

Peter knew nothing about her was real from the first moment he spotted her hurried steps approach him in patent black stilettoes. He sat upright in his seat at reception and checked his watch: 4.18am. Slap bang in the middle of the coma hours: when the occupants of the hotel were dead to the world and the only sound was the ventilator wheeze of the lobby vending machine.

He realised the lush platinum blond tresses were a wig, her pretty features were a silicon mask, and the hourglass figure under the scarlet wrap-around dress was likely due to a girdle and padding, yet when she stood before him, laid her warm hand upon his, and in a breathy, shaken voice said, "Please, can you help me?" he knew he would do whatever she asked.

"Oh yeah, the circus is coming to town, Petey boy," Ron drawled as he slammed into the seat beside Peter at the weekly staff meeting. Ron had pitched his voice just loud enough so Mr Aldridge could hear him, and Peter noticed the crease of annoyance on his boss' face. Ron nodded a defiant hello at Aldridge, and chewed his gum loudly.

"Are we all here?" Aldridge asked, scanning the room. The staff members idling by the coffee machine shifted reluctantly, cups in hand, and slid into their seats.

Ron winked at Peter, and lowered his voice a fraction, "Ten bucks it's a freak show. Otherwise he'd leave it to Lucy to give us the skinny."

Peter nodded politely, but wished Ron would quit

acting like they were buddies. If there was anyone on the staff he wished he could see less of it was Ron, yet they were always assigned shifts together.

Aldridge cleared his throat. "Before I hand over to Lucy to go over this week's schedule, I want to add a few words about a special group staying with us this weekend. The Aldridge Arms has always welcomed guests who represent alternative lifestyles. We've built a reputation for offering folks a space where they can mix with others of their mindset without condemnation or judgement. They're customers, just like any other, except they... ah... express themselves differently."

Ron sorted derisively. Peter edged away from him a little to avoid the full wattage of Aldridge's disapproval.

"This weekend we're hosting the..." Aldridge looked under his glasses at a sheet in his hands, "... Carnivdoll, the mid-West's largest celebration of rubber dolls and their fetishists." Aldridge paused. "I understand this is going to be a new concept to many of you, but to sum up, these folks like to dress up in full latex bodysuits, including masks."

Ron sat up in his seat, and murmured, "What the fuck?"

"We've had BDSM groups stay here before, so we've all seen some outlandish costumes over the years. This is no different. Remember, respect and good manners are the bedrock of our business. As long as they abide by our rules and regulations, every single one of them will be met by courtesy and kindness from each member of staff." He skewered Ron with a direct stare, "Understand?"

Ron smirked at Aldridge while everyone else responded with a chirpy assent.

"Now, Lucy is going to fill you in on the exact schedule of events. Plus, she'll explain some of their lingo and terminology, and hand out written information. Please pay attention, because it'll cut down on misunderstandings. Give them a nice Aldridge Arms welcome and we'll have no problems."

Throughout the rest of the meeting Ron fidgeted as if he had a bad itch, and on the way out of the room he let loose his invective on Peter. "Aldridge has gone too far this time. Does he even consider himself a Christian?"

"Doesn't the bible say we shouldn't judge –"

"It doesn't fucking say 'Thou shalt dress up in rubber doll suits'!"

Peter recoiled slightly at the language. He hadn't been brought up to talk like that. Maybe in the bar, after a couple of beers... but not at work in the middle of the afternoon. But Ron was from the East Coast and didn't believe in withholding his opinions.

Ron's cheeks reddened, "I mean... That's some fucked up shit. What kind of pervert needs to do that?"

Peter shrugged and glanced away, hoping his face wouldn't reveal anything Ron could seize on.

"Christ! And Aldridge's preaching at us like he's so almighty perfect. If those gimps weren't paying top dollar Aldridge wouldn't give them the steam from his piss!"

Peter zoned out the ensuing complaints, but over the next week the event was all that Ron could talk about. During one night shift together he showed Peter links to online videos.

"They call themselves maskers," Ron said, as he dawdled by the hotel desk during the coma hours. Ron was the Night Duty Manager, so Peter had to humour him. Usually Ron goofed off, smoked cigarettes outside, or watched TV in the duty manager's office. Peter preferred it that way. It was better to be stuck with all the work than to endure Ron's constant patter. Peter was pretty sure Ron did some other substances occasionally, as he sometimes burst out of his office, revved up and strangely antagonistic. Yet, at will, Ron could switch on a sleazy charm and be as nice as pie to a customer. Peter had seen people fall for it again and again, and later Ron would laugh at them.

"Here, this one explains how the dudes get into their femsuits..." Ron said, elbowing Peter. "Look, they have a pouch to tuck away their dicks!"

Peter winced as he glanced at the silent video of a lean man demonstrating how to squeeze into a silicon bodysuit to transform himself into a rubber doll woman. Then Ron flicked onto a gallery of images and scrolled through them with his thumb, commenting on the exaggerated features of the doll faces and figures.

The invective went on like this for days, until Thursday night when Peter got fed up with it.

"Don't you think you're a little... obsessed with this stuff, Ron?" he ventured, after another ten minutes' lecture on the costumes and habits of the fetishists.

Ron's face flushed. "What're you implying?"

"I don't know, maybe you should call in sick this weekend if these people offend you so much."

"And miss the show?" Ron grinned wide. "No sir. I'm expecting to be entertained every night. I'm gonna charm the tips offa these pervs."

He barked a laugh, and leaned in close as if he was offering Peter conspiratorial advice. "Weirdoes love it when you treat them like normal people. These guys lay out thousands for their rubber suits, so I reckon they'll be inclined to tip a sympathetic manager." Ron put on an expression of fake sensitivity that made Peter's stomach roil.

Ron tapped his cheek. "Yeah, I got my mask too."

He drummed both hands on the counter in anticipation. "I'm gonna have fun this weekend! I plan to take plenty of pictures on my phone. Maybe I'll post them online afterwards. I wonder what their wives and kids'll say when it comes out they dress up like sissies."

Peter suppressed a surge of fear, and said, "Well you better not let Aldridge find out, or you'll lose your job."

Ron waved Peter's warning off. "I'm not worried. I'm the master of the anonymous account."

Peter pinched back his disapproval, hating himself. A few minutes later Ron finally retired to his office, and the welcome comfort of the night shift quiet settled over the lobby. The glass doors and bright lights barred the enveloping darkness. In these rare moments of peace Peter relished the solitude and imagined being the captain of a dreaming ship forging through the night.

He leaned forward in his chair to tap the desk monitor, and the fabric of his trousers rubbed against the French silk knickers he wore underneath.

A blush rose in his cheeks, and he inadvertently looked over his shoulder to check that Ron was still in the office. As if he could see or guess what Peter wore underneath his clothes.

Peter loved the sensation of silk against his skin. More than that he adored wearing women's lingerie, stockings, and shoes. No one knew about this. Especially not his two football-obsessed brothers, or his friends from college. It was a secret he had guarded with diligent care, always assured of the shame it would bring should he be discovered.

One time when he was four he had dressed up in his mother's frilly babydoll nightdress, and staggered about in her pumps, feeling pretty and incredibly happy. When his mom discovered him she burst out laughing, and hugged him to her chest. The warmth and happiness drained away at the sound of his father's footsteps. All Peter remembered was shouting, the roughness of his father's touch when he pulled the clothing off Peter, and the stern warning to "*Never do that again!*"

His parents didn't mention the incident after that, he wasn't even certain they remembered it, but for Peter this had been a thunderbolt moment. His love of dressing up in women's clothing never waned, but from then on it existed inside a cocoon of fear and shame.

He knew there were other men like him, cross-dressers,

but he could not imagine going outside wearing women's clothing. It prompted overwhelming anxiety. The most he could do was lock his doors, draw the blinds, and dig out the special trunk of items he kept, padlocked, under his bed. Then he could have his own fashion show, and experiment with makeup.

When he felt brave he wore one of his favourite pieces underneath his work clothes, and savoured the delicious terror of having his true self so close to the surface. Ron's stream of jokes about the rubber doll fetishists had promoted him to wear lingerie under his clothes every day that week.

Peter did not feel any draw to wearing a femsuit. He'd wondered if discovering this underground scene would unearth any buried fantasies, but he discovered no attraction to rubber or latex, which seemed cold and unyielding to him. He preferred the direct contact of clothing on his skin. He wanted to be a man yet have the freedom to dress as a woman.

But he envied the people who would be attending Carnivdoll – their courage to do what made them happy, no matter how it veered off the straight track everyone else seemed forced to travel on.

Peter yearned to be courageous enough to go to one of the clubs or bars in St. Paul where he would be accepted, or even put up a profile on a cross dressing dating site. Yet every scenario he imagined ended with him running into someone from his hometown, which inevitably resulted in the loss of respect from his dad, brothers, and possibly his mother. And what would his co-workers say? His chest constricted just thinking about it.

Peter stood up suddenly to interrupt his thoughts. It was foolish speculation. He had accepted his life the way it was now: guarded, but safe.

One day, he might break his self-imposed restraints, but this weekend he would admire the free from the sidelines.

Peter looked at the face of the woman in front of him, feeling the warmth of her hand on his. Her eyes were large, and a startling blue. They summoned the image of a spring river under a thin veneer of ice. He could almost hear the rush and bubble of water cascading over rocks, swollen from melting spring snow. Her mask was glued expertly around the eyes. It was seamless, far better than anything he'd seen that weekend. Everything about her seemed *real*, except she was clearly wearing a silicon mask.

"Your name, miss?" His training kicked in. First off establish if she was a guest, and her room number.

"Valerie," she said. Her accent was light, perhaps southern. "I'm in the Brigitte Suite."

That was the most expensive room in the hotel, which meant Peter had to give her the most discrete and professional service. He tapped the screen with his left hand and saw her full name: Valerie Palmer. She was booked in for five nights, and had paid in full.

"I'm Peter Witt. How can I help you, Miss Palmer?"

Her grip on his hand tightened a little, and he looked back into her expressive eyes.

"Please, it's Valerie... Miss Palmer sounds so formal."

On impulse he placed his free hand over hers as a reassuring gesture.

"Valerie, how may I help?"

She paused, the urgency knocked out of her like sails collapsing from a change of wind, and glanced down at their hands. He took it to signal embarrassment - he'd seen this scenario before.

"Is there someone else..?"

She nodded, her luxurious curls bouncing. "In my room."

He wondered which pronoun to use. "Is the person ill?" It was not unusual for an older guest to die, especially early in the morning. And once or twice they had been in the arms of a beau.

"He's unconscious."

Peter tried to move his right hand to reach for the phone. "I have to call an ambulance."

"No!"

Her distress was acute, so much so that it squeezed Peter's heart. He almost gasped.

"He's not hurt, but passed out. I need to move him back to his room before anyone notices. I don't want to embarrass him."

Or yourself, Peter thought.

"I can go to your room and assess the situation. If I need to call for an ambulance, I must."

She nodded, withdrawing her hand - he felt a *pang*. "Of course, whatever you think is best. I just hoped to avoid any... upset."

He looked around quickly. There was no sign of Ron. He'd been absent for hours. Most of the night he'd been 'supervising' the colourful dance party in the ballroom. Much to Peter's irritation Ron, had outdone himself in the charm department and had won over most of the guests. Last Peter had seen of him, Ron had been smooth talking the final stragglers in the bar.

Peter decided not to inflict Ron on Valerie.

He moved around the desk and indicated with his hand. "After you Miss... Valerie."

She smiled.

Peter blinked. Her lips moved so naturally into an expression of gratitude. The mask must have been custom-built for her (his) face. The latex moved with every nuance underneath.

She moved off and walked before him to the elevators. He marvelled at her easy stride in the heels, and the sway of the material. Her outfit was sexy yet classy, not an easy combination to pull off. Peter had studied many celebrities over the years to ponder how to achieve that effect.

She glanced back to check on him, and for an instant he forgot everything except her vulnerability.

They rode the elevator to the second floor in silence. Valerie's step quickened as they walked along the south wing until they reached the white marble entrance hall. She swiped her card, and Peter followed her into the living room of the suite. One wall was made entirely of glass, and during the day it offered a spectacular view of the lake. The suite stood on metal stilts, and had a large balcony, its own private driveway, and access from the outside. It was popular with honeymooning couples, and was booked out constantly despite the steep price tag.

Flames flickered in the modern fireplace. Jazzy music played in the background. An empty bottle of red wine stood on the oak coffee table, along with two glasses containing its dregs. A man lay slumped on the right-hand side of the large, white brocade couch, his head titled back. He wore a shiny black latex mask with holes for the eyes, nostrils, and mouth, a white shirt with a tie, and trousers. One of his loafers was kicked off as if he'd been hit by electricity.

Peter moved quickly to the man's side, rehearsing his first aid training. The man was breathing deeply. Peter checked the pulse: strong and slow. He seemed asleep.

Peter noticed a white residue at the nose, and frowned. He glanced over at Valerie. She stood before the fireplace, and grasped her hands together.

"Is he all right?" Her voice trembled a little.

"From what I can tell. I'll try to wake him."

Peter addressed the man in a loud, clear voice, "Sir, you have to go now."

No response.

"Can you hear me?"

Peter placed his hands upon the man's shoulders, and lightly shook him. "Sir, please open your eyes."

A loud snore erupted.

The ridiculous noise inspired a burst of laughter from Peter.

He straightened up and turned to Valerie, still smiling. "He's stoned and unconscious. It might take a while to wake him. How did this happen?" As soon as the words left his mouth he realised it was an improper question.

"Oh," she said, "we met tonight. I don't do this normally..." she trailed off.

Peter stepped towards her with his palms out in a calming gesture. "You don't have to explain, it's none of my business —"

She raised her head and looked at him directly. "I don't get away very often." She said. "Not like this. A little sip of freedom is a powerful drink for a parched soul."

That statement was so unusual and profound that it stopped Peter. No one he knew spoke like that.

"It's intoxicating," she continued. "You believe you can just *be* who you really are. And you forget. All the other things that normally stop you behaving this way. You imagine those rules have disappeared."

She stepped towards him, and shook her head ruefully. "Really, you *pretend* they don't exist." She sighed. "Reality always rushes back in." Valerie nodded at the man on the couch.

"I just wanted that *taste*..."

"But, those rules, they were made up by other people." Peter couldn't believe he was saying this to her. "Is it wrong to express who you really are?"

She moved closer to the man on the couch, and beside Peter. "If it hurts someone else, then isn't that a problem?"

"I think this guy's problem is that he was drinking, and snorting coke. You probably added a little too much excitement to the mix."

Her laugh was champagne bubbles on the tongue. She touched his arm. He fizzed.

"You're very kind, Peter."

His name on her lips was a benediction.

He looked in her luminous eyes, and again heard the gushing of water. Or perhaps it was the blood in his veins.

She raised her hand and touched his cheek. "You have a special insight," she murmured. "So different from this man."

It hurt Peter that she even mentioned the man passed out on the couch.

She stepped close to him, and his arm rose up to encircle her small waist. The music seemed louder. They swayed together, her breath warm on his cheek.

"You have depth and complexity inside you, hiding behind your mild features and combed back hair."

In response he pressed her body against him. There was nothing artificial to her warmth and the kindness in her voice.

They were beside the couch, and as one they sat down. The man behind Peter, snorted loudly, as if he was waking, but settled back again.

Valerie's fingers stroked his hair, and then tousled it. She smiled, showing an even row of small teeth. "I see you, Peter Witt."

Something cracked open inside. A burst of rare emotion paralysed him, and she pressed her forehead to his, until there were only her glacier eyes filling up his view.

"Oh yes," she whispered.

He couldn't breathe. Air vanished. The rushing became a pounding. But the blinding blue eyes kept him fixed.

And he heard, *No, Valerie*. Resonant, deep voices.

Peter was sitting, gasping for breath.

Behind Valerie, on the balcony, two white masks with no eyes or mouth hung in the darkness outside the glass.

He could not draw breath to shout.

Only a taste, Valerie pleaded.

The masks moved *through* the glass. They were figures

of smoke, except for their blank white faces.

Valerie stood, facing them. *I can't return.*

Enough!

And that sound, if directed, could stop a heart.

Peter shivered, unable to run.

We have indulged your fantasies long enough. You are not one of them.

I can be. After all those centuries of watching, I can now be here among them.

Impossible. We can't allow it.

One of the figures raised a shadowy arm, and grasped Valerie's shoulder.

The mask and silicon suit collapsed slowly, as if air was being let out from a balloon.

The wig tumbled finally, onto the puddle of scarlet clothing and fake skin on the floor.

A form, flickering, and unstable, hung beside the other two.

I will find a way, she said.

An exchange passed between the three - electric flashes among distant thunder clouds.

A charged mist swept over Peter's face and he fell back, unconscious.

Rousing from sleep was like crawling through mud. Each step forward sucked him half way back into the murk, but Peter fought to wake up. It was an imperative. His eyelids flickered open.

He lay on the couch.

Valerie's exterior - the wig and skin - had disappeared.

Groggily, Peter sat up and checked his watch. 4.55am. Only minutes had passed, but it felt like a month.

He stared at the other man, stupidly, trying to remember the progression of events. After a couple of moments memories reassembled and clarity returned.

The image of eerie blank faces floating towards him

arose in his mind, and a jab of fear jolted him to his feet. Somehow, he knew he wasn't supposed to remember anything of what happened.

Peter leaned forward and pulled up the mask over the chin to reveal the face of Valerie's suitor. Ron. Of course it was. His furore had been a cover for obsession and thwarted desire.

Peter pulled his phone out and took a photo of Ron, passed out, with the mask half-on.

Insurance, he thought.

He slapped Ron lightly on the face.

His colleague's eyelids popped open, revealing fearful, bloodshot eyes. He bolted upright. "Where is she?" he shouted.

"Who?" Peter said.

"Val..."

Peter watched the pained expression on Ron's face as he struggled to hold onto the memories slipping away. Then he relaxed, as if he realised it might be better to forget.

"What happened?" he slurred.

"One of the guests on this floor complained about noise. I came to check and found you like this.

Ron grabbed his face and yanked the mask off. "What kind of fucking joke is this?"

"I don't know, Ron. Perhaps you can explain why you were passed out wearing a gimp mask?"

Ron's face reddened, then paled.

"It's nearly 5am. The early birds are going to be up soon. The chef will arrive shortly. We'd better get out of here."

Ron staggered to his feet. "I don't know... I don't remember what happened. I must've been drugged!"

"You should wash your face before anyone sees you," Peter noted.

Ron glanced in a mirror, and wiped the bottom of his nose. He grunted thanks at Peter.

They left the room and returned to the lobby. In the elevator Ron said, "You're a good guy, Peter."

When Peter walked out of the lobby into the car park a couple of hours later, the world outside seemed shockingly bright. He drove home singing along to all the stupid songs on the radio.

After a long sleep Peter woke up refreshed, and turned on his computer.

'Cross-dressing friendly clubs St. Paul' he typed into the search bar, and printed out the list of places, and corresponding maps.

Then he hauled his trunk from under the bed, and hung up the clothes in his closet.

He laid one slinky wrap-around dress over his body and admired himself in the floor-length mirror.

"Valerie," he murmured, and smiled.

Trysting Antlers

Holly Ice

Mugs tinkled in cheers around the bar: the Square had bought another round. He was muscular, solid, but his suit bunched around his ankles. The mirror-shine shoes did nothing to distract from his height but the antlers sprouting from his stubbled head told a different story. Chipped with hairline fractures, they showed he'd been in his fair share of fights. Judging by the smirk and broad, relaxed shoulders, he'd won a few too.

Marilyn ducked down into her wine, avoiding his eyes as he swept the room. She didn't want to start something. He wasn't her type.

The bubbles bounced to the rim of the glass, a soft pockpock of popping candy as they burst and massaged her throat at every sip.

"Hello, ladies."

The voice was smoky and slid over the words like oil. He looked much the same: slick, gelled hair, curled antlers and lithe body sidling up to Square's girl. Marilyn took a big gulp of wine, her eyes opening wide to become blue starbursts as she opened the packet of nuts in front of her: this was going to be good.

"What's your name, sweetness?"

Eyelashes dipped in plea and heels rocking on the tips, the girl turned to Square.

The greasy man turned too. "He yours?"

A nod as she fiddled with her glass, eyes averted, a ruffle in her pink top.

Grease snorted. "I can take him."

Square slammed down his mug, sloshing ale over the brim. It puddled on the bar, reflecting the lights as stars, a mini universe in polished wood. Marilyn crunched a nut. Its wrinkled bark tickled her tongue with salt.

"You what, kid?"

"I can take you."

Square pushed him, forcing him onto his back foot. "Name?"

"Sid." The kid adjusted his stance, feet beneath his shoulders, weight centred and ready. He had guts, she'd give him that. "You?"

"Ron." He clapped his callused hands, dry skin catching, barnacles beneath the new suit and blue cuffs. "You done this before?"

"Yes." Sid stroked a cracked end to an antler. "Couple times."

"Well, you don't know how to pick a fight."

Ron charged, head bowed, and Sid doubled up fast to catch the running points with his own. The crash splintered wood and stools squeaked as folk shuffled back to a safe distance. The dullists' shoulders bunched and twitched as they threw weight behind their charge.

Sid was silent, smirking into Ron's face. Ignoring the power play, Ron grunted and pushed, forcing Sid back a step. Their hands were fisted at their waists, veins raised as they worked their shoulders and thighs. It was going to be a long battle.

Marilyn crunched another nut, riveted by the spectacle.

"Hey."

She didn't turn her head but spared a quick glance. What she saw made her put the nuts down and swivel in her seat. A quick tug at the hem of her top to improve her cleavage, and she was straight to the point.

"Who are you?" She smiled and tilted her head as she waited.

"Kobe."

"Unusual name."

He shrugged and took a sip of his drink; it was almost finished.

Marilyn took the moment to take him in. The thunder of the fight was no more than background noise now. He had long antlers, pointed at the tips and bare of scratches, smooth as piano enamel. His hair was fluffy, black and the whiff of scent she got was citrusy. Broad shoulders and chest, his shirt creased over his stomach, suggesting tight abs.

Kobe smiled and she looked up, drawn to the perfect white teeth and flash of green eyes which promised grass, earth and tumbles. The undergrowth. He laughed, soft, a whisper under the flying bone and growls. Something softer.

"What?"

"Nothing. You were just...enjoying." He laughed again, slow. His eyes watched hers.

She swallowed and smoothed her skirt, flicked a hair away.

"Well, I'm Marilyn."

Kobe nodded and rose to his feet. "You coming?"

She didn't know where he was going but Marilyn stood too, forgetting her nuts and the fight as she followed him out the door.

Yellow light peeked behind Marilyn's eyelids. She opened them to stare up at a strange ceiling and turned to see an empty bed, covers hollowed and chill from his departure. She sat up. The soft satin touched her body in a whisper as it fell; she smiled.

Sweet citrus and the cackle of oil echoed down the hall, so she found her day-old clothes and followed the smell over cold tiles to the breakfast table. Her toes tingled.

"Hey, sunshine."

Marilyn laughed, hugging her pimpled arms, and

hopped up onto a stool. "Breakfast? So kind."

Kobe passed her a plate, complete with two pancakes, and pointed to the lemon juice and sugar on the table.

"Help yourself."

He watched as she ate, rolling up the pancakes one by one and swallowing them an inch at a time with her hands as a guide. The lemon-sugar mix glistened in the sun.

"Interesting."

She snorted and pointed to the other stool.

"Aren't you going to eat too?"

He shook his head. "Already ate."

"Okay." She took her last bite and walked over to him. "Look, I'm really sorry but I've got plans with the girls today. Shopping trip! Need to feed Rupert, too. You mind?"

Kobe shook his head and opened an arm for a hug. "No problem. I'll catch you later. Got your number, remember?"

"Great! I'll just grab my shoes."

"Sure." Kobe took her plate and put it in the sink with his own. "Later."

Marilyn bought a new dress while she was out; backless and short. She changed into it at home once the girls had left and perfected the fit with little tugs.

In the rush, she didn't bother to measure out Rupert's food. She used a cup to pile it into his bowl instead. Having locked him in the utility room, she applied fresh make-up and was ready, her pink lips perfumed gloss.

She set the alarm and headed back to The King's Arms, figuring she'd text Kobe once she settled.

The bar was full and it took some time to get a drink, even with her cleavage. Once she had her wine, she scanned the room. It was a busy night and the pub was packed with smoke. Misted figures roved from bar to table and back. Local university girls littered the usual crowd. They stood out with their short, flattened hair and branded hoodies.

That's when she saw him. Kobe sat by the jukebox next to a redhead in a white, knee length skirt. The two were flirting, her legs crossing and uncrossing once a minute and his finger brushing her nose as they laughed.

Marilyn's eyes narrowed and then shut as she tossed back her drink. She knew what she'd do. No one fucked with her. Smiling, she placed her empty glass on the edge of the bar and left.

The next morning dawned grey and foggy. It was cold out but Marilyn put on the same black dress anyway, complete with heels and pinked lips. It had to be perfect. She texted Kobe, telling him to meet her at the pub, and clicked down the street.

Greeting the bartender, she ordered and installed herself in the same booth she'd seen Kobe in the night before, by the jukebox. It seemed appropriate. There was a glass mug of ale on the coaster next to her, ready for him. The glass spun webbed rainbows over the table.

He arrived fifteen minutes later wearing jeans, a shirt and a smile. Not too early. Not too keen. Relaxed, he weaved through the regulars with a few hellos and high fives as he made his way over.

"Hey."

"Hey." He sat. "This for me?"

Marilyn nodded and took a sip of her own drink. "Yeah. Got it ready for you."

"Thanks."

"No problem." She smiled and placed a leg over his knees. A fingertip pressed a button on his shirt and toyed with it. "You had a good few days?"

He nodded and stroked her cheek. She tried her best not to cringe.

"Sure, been missing you though."

Turning her head, she snuggled into his hand before

taking another sip. "Up to much?"

"Not really. More pancakes, you know." He laughed.

"I bet." She waited until he'd had a good half of his drink before she spoke again. "You want to get out of here?"

Kobe grinned and stood up. He swayed a little. "Already? Sure, let's go."

Kobe was asleep within the hour. The pill had done the trick. Marilyn sat on his chest and pinched his cheek to check he was out cold. No reaction. His skin still rose and fell beneath her. The only sound in the room was his breathing and hers. Intimate. She laughed into his ear.

"This won't hurt but I sure hope you don't get laid after."

She got off him and grabbed her purse, rooting around inside for the tool she'd added before heading to the pub. On finding it, she straddled him again and waited. He still hadn't moved, let alone woken up. Great.

Clenching the base of one antler, she got to work with the mini saw. The bone dusted onto his forehead and collected on his eyelashes like snow. He was beautiful really, she mused. Leaning down, she pressed a kiss onto his mouth and left a pink flush behind. She continued.

The cut was ragged and uneven. It would be obvious he was shorn rather than shed and the thought made her grin. She blew at the dust to better see the cut and chopped through the last of the horn. The dust flew like glitter, bringing the scent of filed nails and stale alcohol; she scrunched up her nose and placed the shorn antler on the bed.

Then she stared at the stump. It looked ridiculous next to the full antler, a midget or stunted dwarf half hidden by his hair. The outer layer under the antler-brown was almost white but the solid pulpy marrow within looked similar to papier-mâché or the whorls of a felled tree. And the felling was all her fault.

Grinning, she sawed on the second horn, relishing each squeak; she didn't want people to think the first was an accident. Kobe had to be de-manned.

Once finished, she stood and dressed. She hid the saw in her bag and took the antlers to the door. Kobe still rested, both eyes peppered white and his features soft under the powder like a painted mask, lips reddened. The antler indents sat empty in the pillow, hollow. Perfection.

Nodding, Marilyn shut the door and made her way home, his antlers under her coat with one arm as she pretended to be cold. No one stopped her.

Home, Marilyn petted Rupert, her giant fluffy Alsatian, and put the antlers on the kitchen counter. They knocked together like a door-knocker.

"Sorry I took so long, buddy. But I've got something for you."

Opening a drawer, she took out a full sized saw and set to work, dividing the antlers into thirty centimetre pieces before placing each fragment in the dog's cupboard.

The last piece she left on the side while she poured a glass of wine and put on the TV. Once her place was set up and favourite movie sorted, she gave the antler hunk to the dog and smiled: Rupert loved his gift. His tongue and teeth were on show, extricating the marrow with the satisfying, primitive sound of tooth grinding bone.

A good week later, Marilyn noticed Kobe in the corner of the pub. A couple of guys were poking his side and peering over his head at the stumps. She could hear their babble.

"What happened to you, mate?"

"Where's the rest of ya?"

Marilyn smiled into her glass and watched the show.

"You shed early or summin'?"

"Nah it's a good month too early."

Kobe met her eyes across the bar. From that distance, they burned black like coal but he didn't make a move toward her. He knew better, now.

He turned to the guy nearest to him. "Let's say I lost a bet."

The guy laughed and clinked glasses with his friend. "Fair few fillies too, huh? You ain't getting laid till they grow back!"

Marilyn finished her wine and pocketed her nuts. She passed by Kobe on her way to the door.

"I had a great night, Kobe. Thanks, but don't call me again."

Laughter, hoots and slapped backs followed her out the pub.

The Honey Trap

Ruth E.J. Booth

"What the hell is that?"

The apple looked awful. A piebald runt in red and yellow-green, with a sandpaper roughness around its bear-stub stalk. A bulge threatened one side of its thick-looking matte skin, squeezing creases into its squat sides. It sat on the table like an insult, a gnarled middle finger to the perfected #04B404 Foods Agency standard that reigned the international markets.

Jack Becker – accredited independent collective operator, award-winning Growth Guru, author, cult TV personality – plucked up the fruit in one rubber-gloved hand.

"I have never," he said, "*ever* seen such a hideous-looking apple before. Truly."

Becker shook his head, and smiled.

"What's your secret, kid?"

The kid shrugged, hands thrust in the pockets of a goodwill grey hoodie, and looked about the Faire. At tables stacked with bespoke preserves, and obscure small town delicacies crammed between avalanches of vegetables; rows haunted by drifts of discerning foodies and brand-stamped hipsters, sizing up each other's loyalties. Becker's own table was bare by comparison, but he was here as the borough's resident Growth Guru, not head of the largest collective this side of the city.

Still. Compared to the fans who usually showed up for his advice, this guy looked more like someone's kid brother. Becker took another glance at the hooded face. Kid sister, rather.

"Hey, Cole." Becker leaned back and hollered at his warehouse manager, the guy with a better eye for varietals than anyone else he knew, buried behind crates of Becker's latest Grower's Guide. "You gotta see what we got here, man, seriously."

"Oh wow, I haven't seen anything like this since the bees died out."

"I know, right? Do you know it?"

Cole shook his head. "I woulda said it was a Calville Blanc, but the colouring's all wrong, and the size, it's *all* wrong." He hesitated to touch the misshapen apple. "Nope. Where did she get this?" Becker shrugged. "Where did you get this?" Cole asked the kid this time, who clammed up and wouldn't budge.

Becker waved off his buddy.

"So you grew this yourself?" he said.

She nodded.

"Okay then."

Becker sat turning the apple in his hand. Maybe the kid was telling the truth. It certainly didn't hurt to try and find out a little more.

"Do you mind if I try a bit?"

Taking the knife beside him, Becker carved an oblique slice off the apple, slid it off the blade and into his mouth. The crisp flesh tingled as it brushed his tongue, like the moment before a lightning strike, and Becker bit down.

Juice billowed into every nook of his mouth – around his tongue, between his teeth – nectarous and sharp, and so alien-strong it was near unbearable. Becker almost choked as he forced himself to chew slow, to savour it.

"That is incredibly sweet," he managed. "I mean, don't get me wrong. I've never seen something so goddamn ugly in all my life, but compared to the agency standard? This just blows it out of the water. Excuse me." Becker took a draught from the glass next to him, swilled and spat. "Okay, wow. That more than makes up for its size. Who would expect a runt like that to pack such a punch?"

Becker caught the smear of juice gathering on his chin, set down the knife to reach for the fresh wipes.

"So, you grew this yourself," he said, as he folded the tissue away. "Why don't you tell me about it?"

The kid said nothing.

"I mean, of course you're using a custom blend of plant food here. Not the flat beer trick, everyone knows that's a myth." He paused for a reaction. Still nothing.

Becker waited. With some of these fans, it took them a while to get an answer out, as if any talent they might have for the art see-sawed their ability to express themselves in words. She just needed a little time to get herself together.

But the kid shook her head. Coy.

"No? So... What? You want me to guess?"

The kid nodded shyly.

"Okay then, let me think…"

Becker threw the kid a few stock questions as he examined the apple once more. The one that couldn't have come from the self-pollinators normal people grew. That broke about a hundred international laws of sale. That a welfare kid couldn't possibly be growing – not an heirloom, surely? Becker rocked the impossible apple between his hands. He could take all the guesses he liked. If you'd told Jack Becker that a kid was growing an apple like this – even if she was as old as he'd been when he'd started, he wouldn't have believed you if you'd stuck it in front of him, carved off a piece, told him to bite... A drop of juice sluiced into his palm, and Becker struggled not to take the glove between his teeth and suck the nectar out of the folds there and then.

Ruckus. Becker's eyes snapped up to a nearby stall. The Bow Boys, broadcasting their latest exclusive, an heirloom find – a lonely, last-of-its-kind, only-for-most-chronically-trust-funded tree, dug up withering in some deserted

Arizona backwater – across a clutch of toothpick-wielding rubberneckers.

He didn't have time for this. Becker clicked his tongue against his teeth, dislodging a piece of fruit in the back of his gum.

"Well, you've got me," said Becker, handing back the apple. "Well done."

The kid smiled and carefully wrapped the apple back in its supermarket bag.

"What's your name, by the way?" Becker asked.

The kid said, "I have to go."

And Becker let her. He thanked her, shook her hand – and on the count of ten, followed the kid out of the community space and into the street.

Outside, the summer crowd at The Temple bar spilled out between faux pear trees on the right-side pavement. To the left, a honeysucker pulled out of an alleyway, and a pair of cops wrestled some waster who'd missed the street composter by a few feet.

Becker cursed his luck and headed back to the table.

"Anything?"

Cole shook his head and continued stacking guides. "She's not a regular. No one's seen her before. We don't know anyone working on anything like that, in ours or any other collective. Assuming she's online, she's well hidden."

"Everyone's online." Becker stripped off the rubber glove with a wet smack and handed it to Cole. "Can we get the mem-sniffer on this one? Take the glass as well." He elbowed aside a pile of books and dug it out. "See what you can find."

"Really that good, huh?"

Cole paused, a recently cultivated tic of disapproval that Becker had learned would go away if he didn't acknowledge it. They both knew who would break first.

"All right then..."

Becker shrugged off the tone. "You didn't taste it. It

was… indescribable. East side couldn't come up with this with a million years and a batch of monkeys."

"Yet you have no clue where it comes from."

Becker dug a slice of skin out of his teeth and added it to the water. "Not yet."

The bell was flat, and it took twenty minutes and another tenant going up to get Becker into the building.

"Hello, Mrs Hoffman, is Danielle available, please?"

A half-moon pair of glasses looked him up and down from behind the door chain.

"Just a moment."

Becker never had cause to be in this neighbourhood. Here the tenement roofs and vacant lots were owned mostly by a revolving chain of pushers, fighting a winning battle against limited police resources and a losing one against the rising salt levels in the groundwater. For now, it was nothing to do with him. The growers kept to their patch, the pushers left them alone. It worked.

The corridor was dark and smelt of too much disinfectant for concrete.

"What are you doing here?"

For someone so evasive, the kid was direct. Becker liked that. He flashed her a photo-op smile. "And hello to you too. Can I come in? I'd like to talk to you. About that apple you showed me."

Grey hood folded round her neck, Danielle Hoffman stared at him.

Mrs Hoffman yelled, "Are you going to let your friend in, or are you going to keep him waiting out there?"

The kid disappeared from view, and the door slid open.

"Come in," said Mrs Hoffman. "I'm sorry about my daughter. She forgets her manners sometimes. Would you like some coffee? Danielle, make your friend a cup of a coffee. Watch out for that machine, the power's on the blink again. Do you take it black or white?"

"Black, please, Mrs Hoffman."

Becker was gently herded between a beaten up sofa and a coffee table, as Mrs Hoffman filled in the blanks that a government sanitation truck registration and a hand-printed doorbell sticker couldn't. The terrible drainage on the lower floors, how it aggravated her health complaints, how he shouldn't take her child's behaviour to mean anything more than her long nights Working for the Government –

"I drive a honeysucker, Mom."

Mrs Hoffman looked askance. "Well *he* doesn't have to know that…"

– and did she park that thing round the front again, and didn't she know that people talked, and why couldn't she be more like her brother who actually had ambition and studied at that *C-U-N-Y*, didn't he know. Becker tried to shoot the kid a sympathetic look. It was the same song of disillusionment he'd heard from scores of misunderstood growers he'd given a home to over the years. Becker knew the key changes by heart.

Danielle clanked down a mug of coffee on the table in front of him and stood there with arms folded.

"You've been following me," she said.

"You're not easy to track down, kid." Becker smiled and indicated the seat cushion next to him. Standing there, she didn't look like a Danielle to him, more like a Dani. Dani Hoffman. Now that suited her better, he thought. Dani didn't sit down. "I don't want you following me." She shoved her hands in her pockets. "I don't want you here."

"Very well." Becker got up. "But imagine all this from my perspective. You show up, out of the blue, with an apple that looks like the bride of Frankenstein and tastes like heaven itself. I ask around after you, but none of the growers have seen you before. There's no blog, no connections. Just the most beautiful piece of fruit I've ever tasted. You'd have to forgive me for wondering what the mystery is about."

The kid shrugged and shifted on her feet. "I just grow apples," she said. "Mostly apples." "Well," said Becker. "Can I see them?"

It was rightly half a bedroom, a dry wall splitting the differences between Dani Hoffman and her brother – more than just age, going by the pounding bass shaking the dust. A single bed, floor stacked books – a copy of the Guide – topped with headphones, and a handful of bottles huddled from the maze of tubes that lined the walls; a complex of homemade pods lashed together with what looked like old guttering, myco-meal tubs and plastic ties. Here and there she'd stuck clippings, taped printouts of sunlit spruce and vast grasslands from the last of the gov-mandated reserves. Explosions of green shoots lined the pipe between feeders – old soda bottles, filled with what looked like high caffeine energy drink. A gamer's basement ant farm.

Becker nodded his appreciation. Of course, structure-wise, there was nothing to mark the kid out from the thousands of fresh-faced foodies he saw at the events, who dedicated precious inches of their cramped apartments to their obsession. Accomplished work for a self-build, certainly, but nothing as promising as what he'd tasted the other night.

"You wanted to see the apples," said Dani.

Becker had missed the six pots underneath the hanging maze, each with its own dwarf apple tree.

"That's not real compost, of course."

The kid shook her head. "Leftovers, garbage mulch, solution. The usual."

She nodded at the wall. At this entire labyrinth of hydroponics she'd built from scratch, just to grow leaf mulch for the apples. Becker whistled.

He bent down and smoothed one of the leaves between his fingers. More of the feeders were set into the soil of each apple tub, drip-feeding the trees. This had to be it. Cole's 'sniffer had come back with the usual traces from the apple fragments – a higher ammonia content than normal, yes – but it was a blunt instrument after all, only able to detect what it was tuned for. Gently, Becker twisted a bottle to get a better look at the label – a neat K, written in marker, and along the line M,S, N, C, and V. Potassium, Magnesium, Sulphur, Nitrogen, Carbon... V had Becker stumped, but he could check that one later.

"So you're experimenting with solutions," Becker said. "That's pretty cool. Have you read Aaron Goldstein's blog? He's affiliated with our collective. He does some really great stuff with blends, you two should meet. We'll hook you up."

"Maybe," said Dani.

Becker bristled and straightened up. He'd just have to try another angle. The kid liked the direct approach, after all.

Becker asked, "That apple you gave me the other night, which one was that from?"

The kid hesitated, then pointed to the M. Becker lifted a branch to find a cluster of shabby grotesques, kin to the apple she had brought that night – then realised so too did every tree, right along the line.

"What suspension are you using, anyway?" said Becker. "This looks more like energy drink than anything else."

At this, Dani Hoffman broke into a smile. She closed the bedroom door, and then went over to the detritus by the bed. Kicking aside a handful of plant syringes, she picked up one of the spare feeder bottles, already brimming. Dani unscrewed the top and held it out to Becker.

He took a short sniff. "Holy shit," he recoiled. It stunk like the composters on the street corners.

"Have you been...pissing on your plants?" Becker said as Dani rocked with silent laughter. "Isn't that kind of dangerous?"

Dani shook her head. "I rigged our poster," she said. She pointed to another mason bottle in the corner, another pile of tubes. "Changed up the strength."

"No burning." Becker nodded. "But I don't get it. I mean, you're a driver, right? Rather than all this, wouldn't it be simpler to just sort of skim the manure off your honeysucker, put that in with the mulch?"

"That's spoken for." A shadow flickered across Dani's face for a moment. "Security's tight. Quotas, clearance checks, sensors."

"Right. I guess it mustn't be the easiest job in this kind of neighbourhood," said Becker. "I heard about this one guy, last month, got jumped while he was collecting. They got out with his entire truck, three building's worth. Dropped him in the septic tank."

Too late, Becker cleared his throat, to make way for an apology, but she just shrugged.

"That's what happens when you get on the wrong side of them."

"The wrong side?"

"You don't cross pushers. You cross them, that's what happens. Don't antagonise them. Keep on their right side. Just keep your head down and get on with it."

"That's what you do?"

"They don't bother me." Dani had pulled her hood back up.

Becker nodded. "I guess you have those new security guards they rolled out for you now, right?"

"Something like that."

"Yeah. Can't afford to lose anything, with the Regen projects out west. Like they say everyone's gotta 'do' their bit," he smirked.

"Yeah." muttered Dani.

Becker tried to trace her gaze from behind that hood. In one corner, a bin sat stuffed with paper ready for mulching. On top, behind a flyer for last week's faire, Becker could make out an array of hastily torn up letters, stamped with the logos of the bigger hypermarkets. The only ones who could afford their own land, regenerated at great expense. The land that sandwiched the meagre reserves, the ones that Dani Hoffman had plastered photos of in every space between the plastic tubes. Field apprenticeships were like gold dust. Rejection slips, not so much.

He changed the subject. "So you're a plumber too?"

"Public convenience maintenance. Only advantage of the job."

"Wait," said Becker. "You became a shitsucker just to rig all that up to your toilet?"

"Why else would I get a job with *GovSan*?" Dani scoffed, possibly a touch too loud to Becker's mind, flatteringly so.

Becker stood back and took in the room again. Dedication, that was what he wanted from his growers. All this effort, this work – evidence of a sharp mind, sure. Life had thrown so many obstacles in her way – her upbringing, her environment, constant rejection – and Dani had just kept on pursuing her dream. But this wasn't just dedication to a craft. More than that; she'd done whatever it had taken, just to get even a fraction closer to her goal. Even Becker had to admit that her single-mindedness was terrifying.

And look at the results. Becker was standing in a stinking goldmine. The first collective that found her was going to make a mint.

The Bow Boys weren't going to know what had hit them.

"Have you ever worked with full scale trees?" asked Becker.

She laughed. "Who does?"

"We do."

Becker watched the kid go back to tending the mulch plants, too nonchalantly.

"It's purely an experiment for now," Becker continued, "trying to see if we can scale up some of our heirloom operations with grafts from miniatures. Maybe," he ventured, "you should drop by some time, take a look."

Dani paused. She lifted an apple from one of the trees on the floor – the K solution one – and looked at it.

"Maybe I could," she said.

Becker nodded. "Maybe I'll see you tomorrow, then."

A voice hurled up from some elsewhere in the apartment. "Danielle, your friend'll be here to take you to work soon."

She turned to him. "You better go."

Becker closed the door behind him, and allowed himself a smile. He pulled out his phone and voice-dialled Cole. Not interested, he smirked to himself. And to think, he'd almost let the guy talk him out of coming over here.

"Are you one of them foodie types? Growers?"

Becker cancelled the call, to find Dani's brother staring back at him behind swollen eyelids.

"Do me a favour, yeah? Tell my sister to just stop growing that shitty dead food and grow some weed instead, man. That shit's way too expensive these days. Even LSD's cheaper now."

Becker raised an eyebrow. "I'll bear that in mind."

"Do that, brah. Man cannot live by fruit alone, you know what I'm sayin'?"

"Well, he seemed nice." Mrs Hoffman watched her daughter as she raided the kitchen cupboards.

"Mm."

"Have you known each other long?"

"Stop trying to set me up with people."

"Who's setting you up?" Mrs Hoffman was innocence incarnate. "You seemed to be doing quite nicely on your own. Although maybe next time you let me wash that sweater first, eh?"

"Mum, look." Mrs Hoffman winced as the girl pulled her greasy hair into a fresh ponytail. "He's not my boyfriend. He talks too much, asks too many questions. He shouldn't have even come here. I had it all worked out and then he... ruined things."

"If you say so. You know, just because he makes the first move doesn't mean it's all ruined. Things don't go the way you planned, doesn't mean they can't still work out. By the way, that package arrived for you." Mrs Hoffman watched her daughter slide the package across the table, and leaned over as she started to open it.

"Nothing to do with you."

"Right. I'm only your mother, Danielle."

"I told you not to call me that." She kissed her on the cheek. "I'll be back late. Don't follow me out. Please."

Mrs Hoffman crossed her arms as she watched her daughter leave. "Well, you remember what I said about that sweater!"

It was just another 80 degree day in the city when Becker found Dani, hood still up, standing outside the Old Factory buildings.

"Aren't you kind of hot?"

Dani shrugged. "Keeps the sun out of my face."

Becker had settled on highlights from the Gold tour for Dani's visit; the promotional spiel that he gave personally to only the most I of the VIPs who saw the Collective's base of operations – or the somewhat I, anyhow. There was a quick stop at what he called their 'guests', a carefully curated selection of companies he felt really got the Collective's ethos and, naturally, understood that joining was in their best interests – the African chocolate warehouse, the handmade pasta company, the recycled paper press. He threw in a little history of the place, the machinery he'd insisted was left untouched from its former life as a soft drink factory. Of course, Dani remained unmoved, save the "oh" that slipped out as they swung by the old testing lab.

Becker smiled to himself as they shuttered the near-antique freight elevator. This was just the preamble, of course. What he had lined up next was going to blow the kid right out of those scruffy buck store kicks.

"Here's where the magic happens," said Becker, and dragged open the gate.

They stepped into vast space – high cast-iron windows in original warehouse brick, casting motes down onto a complex of metal and ultraviolet lights. Grids of greenery ran at waist height and below in recycled artisanal structures, a collaboration with select designers and architects up-and-coming in the borough. A copse of inflatable ex-NASA airpods stood stalactite and stalagmite, lit by ultraviolet lanterns. A half amphitheatre of strawberry plants hung suspended several feet above a rack of pendulous corn. Along chrome pagodas and screens and looping runners, tubes stuffed with green were tended by the Collective's hand-picked growers. Becker strolled on through. To the kid's ant farm, this was a city of the future, gleaming clear, chrome and white.

"We could have run it automatically, but we really wanted a hands-on approach here," explained Becker. "You know Cole – his baby's the space garden over there."

Cole shook Dani's hand in his gloved one. "How are you? Welcome to HQ."

She stared at the floor. Becker guided the kid on, and away from his partner's raised eyebrow.

"You know Aimee Farelli from the Heirloom Vegan blog? That's her people over there, working with the root veg. And we brought Goldstein on board a few months ago – he's been doing some really exciting things in the medicine patch. You two want to chat?"

The kid was the picture of indifference.

"Maybe later, then. Ah. Now this I really want you to see."

A pair of water tanks rose up from the basement on either side of them. Flickering guppies darted between myriad twisted logs. They – people – rarely got it at first.

Becker had to stop the kid from moving on, indicate upwards where the branching wood began to thicken. Becker watched realisation spread across Dani's face as she took in the roots of a forest of fruit trees, then a canopy that stretched high into reclamation tents in warehouse's vaulted ceiling.

"This is literally the heart and lungs of our operations," Becker elucidated. "The tank pretty much supplies the entire building, and we collect any water vapour from the trees up there. Plus we filter a lot of our emissions through the tents. It's the cleanest point in the whole building. Pretty neat, huh?"

Becker looked over at Dani. The kid couldn't take her eyes off it. Everything was going perfectly. Becker went in for the kill.

"If you were open to the idea," he continued, "you could work right in the middle of this. See that island there? That's where we try out our rarer varieties and heirlooms. Strictly the limited edition stuff, sort of our experimental stock. You could try out what you're working on with some of our dwarves, and then scale up to grafts. You'd be working right here, in the oxygen factory. What do you think?"

Dani wasn't looking at the trees any more.

"Are you okay?"

She muttered she was fine, and that she just needed a minute, but it was bullshit, because 'minute' only had two syllables last time he checked. Becker watched Dani sink, back against the glass tank, ribs hefting like bellows and eyes screwed tight.

Becker said, "Uh, do you want to get some air? Let's go out on the roof."

The metal door popped open like a seal, and the oxygen high of the factory's insides gave way to something more steadying. Up here, far enough from choked smog and smouldering tarmac, the air reached a pleasant neutrality. Becker made sure the kid's panic had eased off a little, before he walked out onto the roof. Afternoon sunshine glinted off a handful of drone deterrents, keeping watch for any birds or squirrels the cayenne pepper didn't scare off. Over by the sweetpeas, a couple of yellow-coated 'Bees' were brushing blossoms with fresh pollen. Becker told them to take ten, and went back to his prodigy.

"Better, right? You had me worried for a moment there."

Dani was breathing deeply. Becker figured he might as well spiel while he was here.

"We inherited this garden from the last people who owned this building," he said, "and they inherited it from the original owners. It's sort of a tradition."

But Dani wasn't really listening. She was walking out amongst the spindles and plant pots, sniffing blossoms. This was nothing by the standard of city growers, just a handful of things you might have seen in allotments and roof gardens a few decades ago. She walked around the place slowly, quietly, like the penitent in a house of worship, muttering about soil under her breath.

She stopped at a large raised bed that Becker kept planted with wild flowers.

"Oh yeah," said Becker. "I guess you've read that this is the last patch of open grass anywhere in the city now, what with the grower's ordinance."

Dani hesitated by the edge of the box.

"I'll take it," she said.

Becker was caught off-guard. "Excuse me?"

"The job you offered me." Dani near-as strode over and reached out a hand. "I'll take it."

Becker smiled widely.

"Well, cool," Becker took Dani's hand and shook it. "Very cool. You know what? We should celebrate – with something appropriate, though. Maybe we should get some of the wine up here. We've got this great apple wine we made in collaboration with Asclepius a couple of years back…"

Dani had reached into a pocket and pulled out a pair of apples.

Becker laughed. "Perfect, why not?"

Becker took one and raised it awkwardly up in the air.

"To new creative partnerships." He took a bite and said, chewing, "You know, I thought maybe you weren't interested for a while there, but I think this could be a really interesting collaboration. I can't wait to see what you and Adam come up with, truly. I think we could really give the East side a run for their money in a couple of seasons."

"I'm not interested in the money."

"Of course you're not, you're an artist," said Becker. "Don't worry, we'll take care of all that. We just want you to be free to focus on what you do best."

"And what's that?"

Becker laughed again. "I mean, we can give you everything you need to realise your potential here. Out of that cramped apartment, space to work, away from that job, the pushers. Everything you could possibly need. New varieties to work with…"

Becker was halfway through outlining the results of their hybrid breeding cycle when he noticed Dani watching him, like a sprinter waiting for a gun to go off. No, like a scientist with a laboratory rat. The look she'd had in her room that day, when he'd watched her tend those apples.

"You know," he said, "this tastes a little different from that last one you gave me. What did you put in it?"

"Ketamine," said Dani.

Becker dropped the apple. *Ketamine.* The consonants felt odd in his mouth, his tongue and teeth like an hour after dental surgery. Becker tried to move his hands, watched them flex, disconnected, in front of him, as if grasping at the memory of the apple in his hand.

Standing was a bad idea. Becker tried to steady himself, grabbing at a raised bed as he lowered himself down. The edge felt like a million sawblade splinters dragging through his skin, yet no pain followed the sensation through. Something was in the way. One hand slipped, and it took him a moment of refocus to see that it was bleeding.

Becker sat heavily. How could he have been so stupid?

Then, reality tore into shreds.

Here was sound, in two – a rumbling tattoo, and a buzz, a hum that pulled static. Over here, the bright red lines in his hands, thrown into relief by the raised beds, rendered in pixelated grids that ran across the skyline and to infinity. Scent disintegrated. Becker tried to drag the pieces back into line as the picture fell sideways. Somewhere near, a bulbous shape carved over the stuttering slats of a bed. The apple, fallen, vacillated between a pinprick in the void and an eclipse of the world entire, pulsing out of sync with the voice somewhere behind him.

"I asked you if you were sure about this, didn't I?"

It sounded like Cole. Like him, but as he hadn't been in years.

"I told you she wasn't interested. I told you not to go. And now look at yourself. Lying there like some drooling smackhead."

Becker tried to turn, to answer, but felt his back come against the side of the box. A humanoid shape twisted in front of the 8-bit landscape, warping as it closed in.

The voice shifted, perverse.

"You were too busy thinking of the strapline, weren't you? Another name on the wall. Another Jack Becker success story."

And again. "How else did you think she'd managed to avoid the pushers?"

"Of course they were in on it."

"Of course she didn't care about the Collective."

"All she could possibly need."

The thrum resolved to a thudding, like giant footprints on stone. The pushers, had to be. Invasion over that pixelated skyline, come to destroy what had taken him a lifetime to build. Becker could hear them now, that pound-pound-pound against the rooftop thumping. But, from where his mind was now, that was far back down the tunnel. Back where his useless body could do nothing to stop them laying waste to everything he'd worked for. Assuming he did still give a shit about it. The tunnel twisted and something sloughed from Becker, tight and crawling, as light opened up ahead. Thank God, he thought, he'd be too far out of it to see it happen.

Gently, Danielle Hoffman moved Jack Becker into a recovery position on the floor, and checked his mouth again for any remaining pieces of apple. The panic that had gripped his face moments before had melted into dumb pliability. She checked her watch. Only a few minutes, at best, 'til Becker's pollinators came back. They would have to be enough.

Satisfied, Elle walked back between the rows, arms outstretched and wide, to drift across the fronds as they swayed.

At the box of wildflowers, Elle stopped. She untied her scuffed shoes, leaving them side-by-side at the box edge, as she climbed into the grass. For a moment, she just stood there, savouring the touch of the blades between her toes. Then she lay down on the grass, spread her arms and closed her eyes.

Elle listened to the lazy buzz of the drones above. The whine and bark of cars, once so close and overwhelming, were just a half-heard whisper, like the fading remnants of a dream on waking.

Elision

Benjanun Sriduangkaew

In the clip she flickers and ghosts. The quality is low, audio a
scratch, visuals shot through with artifacts and grain like
ancient oak.

She is dismembered, very slowly. There is no sex, no
lurid spread-eagled limbs on black mattress: this is not
pornography. There is a chair, straight-backed and severe –
it is almost matter of fact, and she sheds no blood as she
comes apart.

One last lingering shot of her scattered around the
room, a pale blunt hand here, a thick calf there, a fistful of
hair, the lower half of a jaw. Brightly painted lips, smiling in
isolation.

The log shows that Kita-Ushma has seen the footage
precisely one hundred and seventy-four times, and that she
has received upward of five thousand copies of the same.
From across the hall, she watches the protagonist of the clip.
In it she wears a long black dress, baring throat and
shoulders like gifts. In person she is sheathed in scales and
icons of the Song, whose notes alone uphold the turning of
stars.

Ashenti Turyen walks the sanctuary, purifying each
clutch of offerings, blessing supplicants. Kita-Ushma kneels
when the priest comes close, gazing at sandals which do not
quite hide toenails like predator teeth. "Revered, I would like
to petition for a song." She holds out a single void pearl
nesting in her palm, stigmatic, smoldering with the shadows
of dead nebulae.

The pearl disappears into the whispering lattice-notes of Ashenti's sleeve. "Of course." She has a liquid, shifting voice, a musical chameleon predisposed by genetics and honed by training to reach almost any range. When the priest's song finishes, Kita-Ushma has an encrypted file in her private band and a key to it in the form of Ashenti's notes.

That sunset she waits in a museum, making a desultory circuit through exhibits of disarmed warheads, guns stripped of their functional intestines, spent scarab shells singed at the edges. When the Song came, war ceased to be necessary; it is almost more procedure than it is worth to acquire carry permits as a civilian not affiliated with temple justice. Kita-Ushma doesn't feel the lack – her part of the city, a mausoleum of entrepreneur hopes, was a gang battlefield pre-Song.

Ashenti emerges from behind a flayed engine, her vestments oddly soundless. She has threaded the void pearl through a slim silver chain, worn around her wrist. "Thank you for seeking me out, Kita-Ushma ul Sadan."

She's prepared for it, but hearing her name uttered by a voice twined to the Song is a frisson that sears the synapses. Spoken rather than sung or she would have been brought to her knees. Kita-Ushma inhales, her heart churning ecstasy. "Does this cause you trouble when all you want is casual conversation, small talk?"

The movement of the priest's eyelashes is slow, considered. "I've tried to curb the effect. There are depressants that'll numb you to it, but I don't recommend them. Breathe to a measure; you will get used to it little by little. I take it you don't attend prayers often?"

"I pray in private." Defensive. "Is it true you can addict people to your voice? Make them do almost anything?"

"Probably. Wielded a certain way it can induce a rush, ping the reward centers, the same as some stimulants do. But this would be abuse of a specialty trained to spiritual purposes, and those of us who can do it are strictly regulated." Ashenti moves her head from side to side, languid. "You've seen the clip. As I understand, it has reached... more pairs of eyes than I care to imagine."

"Yes. The clip keeps turning up, though it'd just be filtered as spam for most. Was it something private?"

"You misunderstand," Ashenti says. "This never happened. It's all fabrication."

"Then why didn't you alert justice units in your temple?"

"The risk to my reputation is unpalatable."

It is not in Kita-Ushma's nature to be unduly suspicious, but to violate the sanctity of a priest in any way – her privacy, recordings of her voice, reproductions of her likeness – is to court destruction of the most thorough category. Suns have died to satisfy holy justice. "They'd be more effective than I am, no? They have access to resources I don't."

"They lack discretion, subtlety, or humanity." The priest wraps the chain around her fingers, lightly rubbing the pearl. "Eight years ago you amputated a Song judge in self-defense. They perished shortly after, being on a remote station and unable to find medical help in time."

"Are you blackmailing me?"

"I'm offering you a fee. I have the power to make the incident disappear completely, so you'll no longer have to look over your shoulder and run from city to city, world to world, at the twitch of a judge's shadow, at the gleam of a vow or the oath of a scalpel. Turn me down and I will simply leave this be, and you won't have lost anything you haven't already surrendered. Work for me and you stand to regain your peace."

Kita-Ushma touches one of the Song's talismans at her throat, a requirement for every Cotillion citizen to wear, titanium-girded cadenzas and diamond mantras. Some mark her as an initiate. "A good cleric would turn me in."

"In our hierarchy there are bonds like the hilt of a sword, and their opposites like the blade, where everything is an edge waiting to cut and draw blood. The person you killed was no particular friend of mine, though neither were they an enemy. I've no pressing cause to avenge them."

She lets go of the talismans. They settle into their places, in rank and file, of choir or army. "Aren't those of the Song meant to be spiritually joined in eternal harmony?"

"Dogma and material reality are estranged partners at the best of times, when they aren't entirely divorced. Even you must realize this much, to have earned the novice's signs." The priest pauses and it is as though there is an interruption of instruments, a melody cut off. "There are zealots, but one mustn't count outliers."

"I'll take the job." Kita-Ushma bites down on the inside of her cheek. Small pains distract. "Your fee's good enough."

Sunrise and she has not slept: she sits in the lobby of an employment agency, cradling a splinted arm, surrounded by drowsy job-seekers. Some are hyper-alert on stimulants, with fluttering hands and glittering eyes. Thin threads of pollutants needle the air, pricking the skin. In the corner a factory worker murmurs dawn chants in an unsteady contralto. The Song marks all things, dividing day from night, hours into minutes: for every chronological delineation there is a verse.

Kita-Ushma waits for a name to be called. Not hers, necessarily, but even under close temple regulations it is not so difficult to appropriate identities from rosters of the dead. When that name pulses on the nearby terminal, broadcasting across the lobby, she stands. Her steps drag and falter as she enters a small office armored by old bulkhead to withstand fire, standard demolitions, and handguns.

The broker takes off her headset, disconnects herself

from a wall socket. "I swear I've seen you as often a man as a woman now. Bit fickle. Doesn't it cost a fortune to modify?"

"I get a discount for being regular." Kita-Ushma sits. The air smells of rust, engine exhaust, red and black spotting the furniture. "I don't ask if being monogendered bores you to tears."

"Broken arm?"

"Not really." Kita-Ushma slips off the cast, shedding it as she would a glove. "Any leads on the file I sent you?"

Gwilin taps her fingers on her left forearm. A mercenary prosthesis mazed with folded blades and slots for ammunition charges, long since inert. "You know this is a terrible idea? The only reason a priest would skip on summoning temple judges is when she has something to hide."

"Good money," Kita-Ushma says lightly, "goes to solid data analysis, not unsolicited advice."

"That clip's circulated outside Cotillion space, not that anyone would recognize your client there. I've traced it back to a lot of infected cortices, entire network clusters scripted to dedicate just enough bandwidth – not sufficient to trigger alarms – to forward this. I haven't been able to find out where the clip originated, but I *did* discover where it first appeared."

"Save the suspense for someone else, friend."

"Testy." The broker gestures expansively with the prosthesis. Servos sing against each other, a modification Gwilin has adopted in place of talismans, which she calls sufficient as far as religious devotion goes. So far she hasn't been fined for her lack of due reverence or sent to indoctrination. "It first turned up on Matharee Station, near the seventh planet in – easy, Kita, don't break my chair."

Kita-Ushma unclenches her hand. "Your furniture's industrial-strength. Matharee Station?"

"Yeah." Gwilin watches her, artificial eyes buzzing.

"Some shithole. Miners' home, mostly lawless. Barely connected, overseen by maybe a couple clerics. The most you could say for that place is you can get away with minor atheism."

"Dreadful," she murmurs and touches her icons. "A cradle of wickedness."

Gwilin sneers at the gesture. "I set out to see if there was a better copy, and actually there *were* lots. The older the copy the better it was. The file's set to... introduce artifacts, damage the audio, each time some condition is met. Every time that happens, other copies would synchronize, degrade to match the same state."

"Specifically what condition?" Kita-Ushma is well aware the footage – not being executable – cannot do that by itself, but given the proliferation, it must be embedded with some script that draws on the resources of each host cortex to accomplish the change.

"I haven't the faintest. *But.*" Gwilin taps a desk projector. "I cross-referenced, made a timeline. For most of its eight year lifetime, this file – this virus – was lossless, perfect integrity. Only recently has it started exhibiting this behavior. I can't be as precise as I'd like, what with temple filters, but I pinpointed the grid addresses as best I could."

Eight years. A shiver razors over her nerves with a torturer's slow affection. "Thanks, that's something to work with, I suppose."

"You *suppose?*"

"It's routine data analysis. Time-consuming, I'm sure, and trying on the patience..."

"My usual fee and no lower," the broker says flatly. "Don't tempt me to charge by the hour."

"No sentiment in you," Kita-Ushma says, but her mind is already elsewhere. A hunch. A pinch of anxiety taking root.

Ashenti returns her call immediately, even though this hour

the priest ought to have been performing an evening rite. "Did I read that right? You want a copy of my passport?"

"Or a log of your travels since –" Kita-Ushma glances at Gwilin's timeline. "Fourteen months ago. Fourteen months, nine days, sixteen hours ago."

"That's very specific."

"Revered, with due esteem, you engaged me to solve a problem."

The priest is holding a bouquet, a haphazard arrangement of ferns and bromeliads: too unpolished to have been a temple offering. She strokes the glossy petals, ringed fingers disappearing between leaves the color of late bruises and midnight prayer. "The logs are yours to peruse. You are the only layperson I've ever permitted such access."

"I appreciate it, Revered." She takes a draw of cigarette, breathes it out, a simmering heat in her chest. The window of her apartment is fogged blue with long years of smoke, warped by weapon fluxes from gang skirmishes. Pre-Song, and so for all intents and purposes – under the theocratic calendar – prehistoric. "I'll get back to you."

Kita-Ushma spent some years in remote places, so remote that he couldn't obtain body modification when he wanted it, so remote his network implants didn't work. It was not a good time, where needs went unmet, familiar comforts were denied; he was desperate enough for surgery access to kill a Song judge. Ashenti saying it was self-defense is only half-right.

Mostly it was an assassination, because sometimes a choice is not a choice at all when the other path is destruction. Kita-Ushma hasn't taken on that kind of work since, has barely laid hand on a weapon, has nearly forgotten how a gun feels in her hand.

She paces the confines of her apartment. Two partitions, the most minute of a bathroom. Once she would have been able to afford better, but eight years ago it took all he had to secure passage from that station, to pay the bribes. He believed, was certain, that his trail had been covered. A change of identity, an erasing of birth signatures, and three years serving at a Song monastery as novice to accumulate certain icons, certain signifiers of devotion. She touches those now, a nervous habit that's time and again resisted breaking. At the monastery –

Dread coils in the depths of her gut. There are particular details, on that station, eight years ago, that she no longer recalls. Novices are reconditioned, slightly, not an indoctrination but there can be lapses of memory. Accidental for the most part. It was a price willingly paid.

Kita-Ushma examines the logs Gwilin compiled, at the one Ashenti sent her. The cross-referencing has already been made as soon as Ashenti gave her access. It's impossible to have a complete set of data; what the broker could obtain on short notice is already exemplary. But the instances of overlap are too many, too often, to be coincidence. Each time the file makes contact with Ashenti Turyen in virtuality, it breaks down a little more.

She takes another draw, goes through the other dozen videos Gwilin found. The same footage – or at least, the same surrounding, setting, format. The face and body change each time. An elderly man with the thick build of an Udendi native. A hard-faced person of indeterminable gender. A bald woman. A teenager, sixteen at most.

Each coming apart, in that same tidy bloodless way, over and over.

On a bad night, and recently all nights have been bad, her part of the city has the look of a fresh battlefield. Commercial boards lie in shards and fragments on the streets; building facades are pocked with blisters and impact wounds. Kita-Ushma can tell they are still alive because they hiss and whisper under a glass storm. In her apartment sometimes the walls, behind their thick coats of paint and steel reinforcements, would throb and twitch. Nerves and tendons as thick as her wrist, geometric organs the size of her thigh. She often wonders why the clergy hasn't cleansed this part of the city, hasn't gathered up the broken pieces and swept them away, the way it has been done everywhere else.

The priests have, at least, suppressed the buildings' signals. Transmitting nerves have been seared and excavated, preventing them from interfering with citizens' connective chips, sending calls for help and imposing such dreams as only foundations and windows might have. When Kita-Ushma first arrived, some of the residential units were still whispering and sending vision-pulses, more white noise than any real trauma, but it made sleeping a chancy proposition.

It would be easy for the clergy to euthanize them, replace them with the urbane buildings bred in approved nurseries, which break silence only to praise the Song and which know no pain. But perhaps this is meant to stand as testament, of what things used to be, of how bad they could be again without theocratic guidance. It draws tourists, pilgrims.

Ecclesiasts visit this area never, judges only to pursue heretics and apostates; that Ashenti agreed to meet here surprised Kita-Ushma. Not that the priest would ever be in danger. The Song cares for its own – her chapter would know, at all times, where she is and react to the first sign of distress.

Half an hour in the damp ruin of a house thick with the acid smell of building-blood before Ashenti shows. The priest's body armor is discreet, but there if one knows where to look: a glint at the wrist, a subtle change in profile. "What did you do in your former life?" she asks, shaking off raindrops made chromatic under the glare of stuttering light.

Kita-Ushma gives the priest a look. The cigarette's heat lingers in her still, wreathing her senses in a mild haze. It might, she hopes, dull the effect of Ashenti's voice.

"Revered."

Ashenti makes a gesture of negation, formal by habit. "I'm sorry, of course I shouldn't ask." She nods at the titanium cadenzas. "Holy service entitles you to privacy for the life you had prior to your novitiate."

"Exceptions being if I've committed crimes against persons of the Song."

"That, yes. What have you found out?" Ashenti receives the extra footage, her gaze briefly distant as she takes the images in. When her eyes refocus, they are wide, her breathing a little quick. "These are all servants of the Song. A sacrament-elector. A lieutenant-sibyl from Springtide Envoi."

"Do they have enemies in common? In common with you?"

"Not that I know of." The priest's voice has gone faint. "But they are all dead."

The shardwine is of no particular quality, but Ashenti drinks it with the refinement of good breeding or long training. She almost imparts sophistication to the wine, the glass, the apartment.

"Have you ever performed indoctrination, Revered?"

The priest holds the wine close, its steam – brine and baked stone – veiling her expression. "Not personally, though I've observed the process. It leaves no lasting damage and doesn't change a person; merely corrects imperfections, controls unruly destructive urges."

"The memory loss," Kita-Ushma says, tries to stay calm. "Can it be targeted? Could indoctrination erase or suppress specific facts or events?"

"I imagine it could." The tone of Ashenti's voice has not changed. But perhaps it is, barely, tense.

"You know about what happened eight years ago, Revered. But how much?"

"In generalities. Who you killed, when, where. Is it

important?"

"Yes." Kita-Ushma doesn't visibly reach for anything, inside her coat or behind her; she's become quite good at making these motions unobtrusive, even to someone giving her their undivided attention. "Who hired me, Revered? To kill that judge. That sacrament-elector. That lieutenant-sibyl."

"That's a peculiar conclusion to leap to, Kita-Ushma ul Sadan."

She is fortified this time – there was more in the cigarette than tobacco – but her breath shudders and her nerves sing supplication. "Not that peculiar. There's a common thread to all this – those faces, I've never seen them, I don't *remember* seeing them. But one, one of them, the woman. She was the judge, wasn't she, the one I assassinated?"

"Is that a confession?" The priest has set down her glass, her face half-obscured in shadow. "That you didn't kill in self-defense but pre-meditated it, for money? For one of my station and purity, my judgment of such things is eminently flexible, but that strains even my reluctance to engage in absolutes."

It has been so long since Kita-Ushma handled a gun. Muscle memory informs her grip and aim; experience plots a trajectory, gives foreknowledge of the exact sound the impact will make, the chair turning over and the heat of blood. How many drops will fleck her skin and clothes, the pattern they would make on the quiet respiring floor. At this range, no armor or shielding will be enough.

"It is a terrible idea, Kita-Ushma, to threaten a priest."

"You aren't going to summon your chapter's judges. With what little rank I earned as a novice, I'm entitled to speak against you before a tribunal. And even if they send me for a complete indoctrination or execution, you aren't going to go unscathed. I was the tool, Revered, but you were the hand."

Ashenti does not move and Kita-Ushma knows why: the priest hardly needs to carry a weapon. "What would you testify with? Half-baked hunches and paranoid fancies are no evidence."

"Suppressed memories," she says softly, "can be recalled. Indoctrination is very exact, so I heard." So she experienced.

"Eight years ago, Kita-Ushma, you were invited to join Elision. For someone as skilled as you to do next to nothing instead of holy service is a waste, almost blasphemy in itself. The invitation stands."

It would be easy, too, she knows that. Become an assassin in service to the Song. Any past misdeeds pardoned, any future ones – so long as they are committed against those outside the hierarchy – preemptively excused. "It was flattering then. It's flattering now. But I prefer to be and act as I am."

"I suppose you would." Ashenti doesn't gather her breath; it is only a slight shift in pitch. Hardly noticeable, unless one knows what to listen for.

Kita-Ushma does not wait for it, a command that might make her turn the gun on herself, that might make her do anything. She pulls the trigger.

Sunrise and she has not slept: she huddles in a tiny cabin on a commercial craft, passage purchased last minute. Dearly bought, but her savings have always gone into emergencies.

It is as the craft docks into a trade refrain that her connection thrums, a distinctive couplet-signature of an ecclesiastic sender. It can't be a judge – an arrest order would have already been carried out before she could enter the port. At the slowest, they would have captured her once she boarded the ship, probably executed her on the spot.

Kita-Ushma delays opening the link, a postponement measured in seconds. She knows she can't put it off any more than she can refuse it.

"Yes," she murmurs, waiting for visual.

A woman, bright-eyed, tattooed at earlobes and jawline: a sestina framing her face. "Congratulations on completing your passage assignment, Kita-Ushma ul Sadan."

Her pulse judders. "You're Elision."

"Quite. I'm your recruiter and sponsor."

The last video. It wasn't Ashenti after all who sent and proliferated it – that was the one puzzle Kita-Ushma hadn't been able to solve. "The Revered," she begins.

"For many obvious reasons she was deemed too poisonous to keep, and hurtling toward apostasy in any case. As I said, you have done well."

"Am I being drafted?"

"Of course not. You enlisted eight years ago. I don't believe we suppressed that?"

"No," Kita-Ushma says slowly. "But Ashenti Turyen did."

"Ah, Falldusk Choir personnel can be so sneaky. Well, technically you've the right to go back on your enlistment." The woman's expression is light, her voice cheerful, and it is just a voice. Friendly. "What will it be then?"

A choice that was not a choice at all. Under the harmony of the Song, perhaps that is the only kind that exists.

"I agreed to it once." She folds herself, presses against the bulkhead. A thin layer, when all is said and done, between her and the oblivion of vacuum. "I might as well agree to it again."

The woman smiles widely, a painted mouth and sestina tattoos moving in precise coordination, like soldiers in ranks, like singers in a choir. "Excellent. I'll be picking you up at the refrain in seventy-two hours. Welcome to Elision, recruit. May the Song grant you a long and faithful future among us."

About the Authors:

Ruth E.J. Booth sold her first short story in 2012, and her most recent work can be found in Fox Spirit's Fox Pockets series. Ruth is also a music critic and photographer, previously published by the likes of *The Independent* and *Kerrang!* (as Ruth Booth). At present, she spends her spare time as a singer, yogini, or half-marathon runner. She can only whistle backwards.

Storm Constantine has written twenty-eight books and well over fifty short stories. Her writing spans literary fantasy, science fiction, and dark fantasy. Storm is founder of the independent publishing house Immanion Press, created in order to get classic titles from established writers back in print and innovative new authors an audience. She lives in the Midlands with her husband, Jim, and five cats.

Frances Hardinge's bizarre, fantastical books are written for 10+/YA, but have an increasing adult readership. Her debut, *Fly by Night* (Macmillan), won the Branford Boase Award, and her other titles include *Verdigris Deep*, *Gullstruck Island*, *Twilight Robbery* and *A Face Like Glass*. Frances is seldom seen without her hat, and is addicted to volcanoes.

Andrew Hook's stories have appeared in *Black Static*, *PostScripts*, and numerous anthologies including several from NewCon Press. 2014 will see the first of two neo-noir crime novels, *The Immortalists*, appear from Telos Moonrise, with the second, *Church of Wire*, due next year. He has recently edited an anthology of punk stories for DogHorn

Publishing, and co-edits *Fur-Lined Ghettos* magazine.

Stewart Hotston spends much of his time trying to make things ex nihilo and then worrying about them while keeping very real people happy. Formerly a proper physicist who now works with complex derivatives, he tends to write speculatively, exploring big issues and how they impact ordinary people – in other words he loves the grand old spirit of science fiction.

Holly Ice studies creative writing at Staffordshire University. She is inspired by the unknown to create science fiction and fantasy stories. Previous work has been published by Indent, Almond Press, the H.G. Wells Festival, as well as in NewCon's recent *Looking Landwards* anthology. She is currently sculpting a fantasy novel and introducing two kittens to her Cotswold home.

Adele Kirby followed a childhood of voracious escapist reading by spending high school voraciously writing escapist fantasy. Writing for pleasure led to a determination to produce a book, and in time she even began to consider begging people to read her work. Adele also meddles at screenwriting, which she adores but gives up annually to 'finish the book'. "Soleil" is set in the same world as one of her spec TV series.

Maura McHugh lives in Galway, Ireland and her short fiction has featured in various venues including *Year's Best Dark Fantasy & Horror*. Her two collections, *Twisted Fairy Tales* and *Twisted Myths* appeared in the USA in 2013. She's written comic book series *Róisín Dubh* and *Jennifer Wilde* for Atomic Diner in Ireland, and was one of the writers of the horror anthology play, *The Hallowe'en Sessions*, which had a sold-out performance in London. Find her at http://splinister.com and on Twitter as @splinister

Jonathan Oliver is the Editor-in-Chief of Abaddon, Solaris and Ravenstone, and the author of two novels and a whole bunch of short stories. He lives in Abingdon with his wife, daughter and their cat.

Stephen Palmer is the author of seven published novels, including *Memory Seed* and *Glass* (Orbit), *Muezzinland*, and *Urbis Morpheos* (PS Publishing). His short fiction has been published by NewCon Press, Wildside Press, SF Spectrum, Rocket Science, Eibonvale Press, Unspoken Water and Solaris. His latest novel, *Hairy London*, is forthcoming from Infinity Plus. Stephen lives and works in Shropshire, UK.

John Llewellyn Probert won the British Fantasy Award for his novella "The Nine Deaths of Dr Valentine" (Spectral Press), and the Children of the Night Award for his short story collection *The Faculty of Terror* (Gray Friar Press). Endeavour has published "Ward 19" and "Bloody Angels" – two crime novellas featuring his pathologist heroine Parva Corcoran, with a third, "Suicide Blondes", due out this year.

Benjanun Sriduangkaew enjoys writing love letters to cities real and speculative. Her work can be found in *Clarkesworld Magazine, Beneath Ceaseless Skies, The Dark,* Jonathan Strahan's *The Best Science Fiction and Fantasy of the Year* and Rich Horton's *The Year's Best Science Fiction & Fantasy.*

noir

The companion volume to *La Femme*

Thirteen stories that dance around genre boundaries but are linked by a sense of foreboding, a prickly itch that will unsettle and leave you with the impression of something sinister lurking just beyond the reach of awareness…

Dark science fiction, the supernatural, puzzling mysteries and shocking twists from:

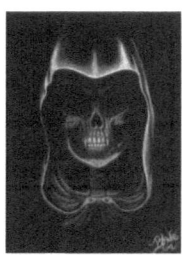

E.J. Swift
Adam Roberts
Donna Scott
Emma Coleman
Paula Wakefield
Simon Kurt Unsworth
Jay Caselberg
Marie O'Regan
Paul Graham Raven
Simon Morden
James Worrad
Paul Kane
Alex Dally MacFarlane

www.ingramcontent.com/pod-product-compliance
Lightning Source LLC
Chambersburg PA
CBHW050907180626
46814CB00007B/2935